"Your daughters were very cute, by the way."

The proud, affectionate look on Noah's face told her he knew he had hit the jackpot when it came to his kids. She could not help but agree.

Wistfully, once again, wished she had a few of her own just like them.

He finished texting. Glanced up, his eyes scanning her face, his expression serious now. "I hope they were polite."

Tess reflected on the three pajama-clad little girls, with their pink cheeks and tousled hair. The three-year-old twins had their daddy's deep blue eyes. Eight-year-old Lucy was lovely, too. Observant and intuitive. Guarded. Aware he was waiting on her reply, Tess said finally, "I think they were more shocked than anything."

He lifted a brow. Urging—no, more like demanding—she go on.

Tess cleared her throat. "Lucy made it clear women did not spend the night at the Welcome Ranch unless they were family." *Which I am definitely not.*

"Ah, well..." He slid his phone into his pocket. "As I said, I'm not looking for a new woman in my life."

That knowledge just left her feeling off-kilter. The way she always did when she allowed herself to want something that was not likely to happen.

Dear Reader,

During our marriage, my husband and I have moved cross-country four times and locally five. What do I hate about it? Packing and unpacking. What do I love? The excitement of finding a new place to live and the joy of making it ours.

Veterinarian Tess Gardner is moving to Laramie, Texas, the place where her family is rooted. She has an exciting new job. And she's inherited a house that is a bit more than what she expected.

Enter CEO Noah Lockhart. He has also moved back to Laramie, in the wake of his wife's death several years before, to be near his family. Life for him and his girls is finally settling down and getting back to normal. Or it will, he is certain, once the latest member of the ranch menagerie is born.

All Noah wants from Tess is help getting through the birth and the first week or two of their new pet's life. In exchange, he will give her a private guest suite and a place to live, rent free, while her house is renovated.

He doesn't expect to get close to her. She doesn't expect to fall for him. But you know what they say about love—it's what happens when you are busy making other plans.

I hope you enjoy this last book in the Lockharts Lost & Found series. If you have missed any of the seven other novels, there is information on Facebook and on my website, cathygillenthacker.com.

Thanks for reading! You, dear readers, are what make all the hard work, creating every fictional family and their stories, worthwhile!

Cathy Gillen Thacker

A Temporary
Texas Arrangement

CATHY GILLEN THACKER

HARLEQUIN
SPECIAL
EDITION

If you purchased this book without a cover you should be aware that this book is stolen property. It was reported as "unsold and destroyed" to the publisher, and neither the author nor the publisher has received any payment for this "stripped book."

HARLEQUIN®
SPECIAL EDITION™

Recycling programs
for this product may
not exist in your area.

ISBN-13: 978-1-335-59444-0

A Temporary Texas Arrangement

Copyright © 2023 by Cathy Gillen Thacker

All rights reserved. No part of this book may be used or reproduced in any manner whatsoever without written permission except in the case of brief quotations embodied in critical articles and reviews.

This is a work of fiction. Names, characters, places and incidents are either the product of the author's imagination or are used fictitiously. Any resemblance to actual persons, living or dead, businesses, companies, events or locales is entirely coincidental.

For questions and comments about the quality of this book, please contact us at CustomerService@Harlequin.com.

Harlequin Enterprises ULC
22 Adelaide St. West, 41st Floor
Toronto, Ontario M5H 4E3, Canada
www.Harlequin.com

Printed in U.S.A.

Cathy Gillen Thacker is a married mother of three. She and her husband reside in North Carolina. Her stories have made numerous appearances on bestseller lists, but her best reward is knowing one of her books made someone's day a little brighter. A popular Harlequin author, she loves telling passionate stories with happy endings and thinks nothing beats a good romance and a hot cup of tea! Visit her at cathygillenthacker.com for information on her books, recipes and a list of her favorite things.

Books by Cathy Gillen Thacker

Harlequin Special Edition

Lockharts Lost & Found

His Plan for the Quadruplets
Four Christmas Matchmakers
The Twin Proposal
Their Texas Triplets
Their Texas Christmas Gift
The Triplets' Secret Wish
Their Texas Christmas Match

Texas Legends: The McCabes

A Tale of Two Christmas Letters
Their Inherited Triplets
His Baby Bargain
The Texas Cowboy's Quadruplets
The Texas Cowboy's Triplets
The Texas Cowboy's Baby Rescue

Visit the Author Profile page
at Harlequin.com for more titles.

This book is dedicated to Ryan, our gorgeous sock-and-mischief-loving yellow Labrador retriever. Thanks for always bringing us our shoes and putting them on our lap when it's time to go for a walk. Don't know what we would do without you, sunshine.

Chapter One

"You're really going to go in there. Alone. Just before dark?" The low, masculine voice came from somewhere behind her.

With the brisk January wind cutting through her clothes, Tess Gardner paused, house key in hand, and turned toward the Laramie, Texas, street. Senses tingling, she watched as the man stepped out of a charcoal-gray Expedition, now parked at the curb. He wasn't the shearling coat-wearing cowboy she had expected to see in this rural southwestern town she was about to call home. Rather, he appeared to be an executive type, in business-casual wool slacks, dress shirt and loosened tie. An expensive down jacket covered his broad shoulders and hung open, revealing taut, muscular abs. Shiny dress boots covered his feet.

Had it been any other day, any other time in her

recently upended life, she might have responded favorably to this tall, commanding man striding casually up the sidewalk in the dwindling daylight. But after the long drive from Denver, all she wanted was to get a first look at the home she had inherited from her late uncle. Then crash.

The interloper, however, had other plans. He strode closer, all indomitable male.

Tess drew a bolstering breath. She let her gaze drift over his short, dark hair and ruggedly chiseled features before returning to his midnight blue eyes. Damn, he was handsome.

Trying not to shiver in the cold, damp air, she regarded him cautiously. Drawing on the careful wariness she had learned from growing up in the city, she countered, "And who are you exactly?"

His smile was even more compelling than his voice. "Noah Lockhart." He reached into his shirt pocket for a business card.

Disappointment swept through her. She sighed. "Let me guess. Another Realtor." A half dozen had already contacted her, eager to know if she wanted to sell.

He shook his head. "No." He came halfway up the cement porch steps of the century-old Craftsman bungalow and handed over his card, inundating her with the brisk, woodsy fragrance of his cologne. Their fingers touched briefly and another tingle of awareness shot through her. "I own a software company," he said.

Now she really didn't understand why he had

stopped by, offering unsolicited advice. Was he flirting with her? His cordial attitude said *yes*, but the warning in his low voice when he had first approached her, and had seen that she was about to enter the house, said *no*.

He sobered, his gaze lasering into hers. "I've been trying to get ahold of you through the Laramie Veterinary Clinic," he added.

So he was *what*? Tess wondered, feeling all the more confused. A pet owner in need of veterinary care? A potential business associate? Certainly not one of the county's many successful, eligible men who, she had been teasingly informed by Sara, her new coworker/boss, would be lining up to date her as soon as she arrived.

Curious, she scanned his card.

In bold print on the first line, it said:

Noah Lockhart, CEO and Founder

Okay, she thought, so his name was vaguely familiar.

Below that, it said:

Lockhart Solutions. "An app for every need."

The company logo of intertwining diamonds was beside that.

Recognition turned swiftly to admiration. She was pretty sure the weather app she used had been designed by Lockhart Solutions. The restaurant finder, too. And the CEO of the company, who looked to be in his mid-thirties, was standing right in front of her. In Laramie, Texas, of all places.

"But even though I've left half a dozen messages, I haven't gotten any calls back," he continued in frustration.

Tess imagined that wasn't typical for someone of his importance. That was just too darn bad.

Struggling not to feel the full impact of his disarming, masculine presence, Tess returned his frown with a deliberate one of her own. She didn't know if she was relieved or disappointed he wasn't there to ask her out. She did know she hated being pressured into anything. Especially when the coercion came from a place of entitlement. She propped her hands on her hips, the mixture of fatigue and temper warming her from the inside out. "First of all, I haven't even started working there yet."

His expression remained determined. "I know."

"There are four other veterinarians working at the animal clinic."

"None with your expertise," he stated.

Somehow, Tess doubted that. If her new boss and managing partner, Sara Anderson McCabe, had thought that Tess was the only one qualified to handle Noah's problem—whatever it was—she would have called Tess to discuss the situation, and then asked Tess to consult on the case. Sara hadn't done that. Which led Tess to believe this wasn't the vital issue or 'emergency' Noah deemed it to be.

More likely, someone as successful as Noah Lockhart was simply not accustomed to waiting on anyone or anything. That wasn't her problem. Setting professional boundaries was. She shifted the bag higher on her shoulder, then said firmly, "You can make an appointment for next week."

After she had taken the weekend to get settled.

Judging by the downward curve of his sensual lips, her suggestion did not please, nor would, in any way, deter him. His gaze sifted over her face, and he sent another deeply persuasive look her way. "I was hoping I could talk you into making a house call, before that." He followed his statement with a hopeful smile. The kind he apparently did not expect would be denied.

Tess let out a breath. *Great*. Sara had been wrong about him. Noah Lockhart was just another rich, entitled person. Just like the ridiculously demanding clients she had been trying to escape when she left her position in Denver. Not to mention the memories of the ex-fiancé who had broken her heart…

Determined not to make the same mistakes twice, however, she said coolly, "You're still going to have to go through the clinic."

He shoved a hand through his hair and exhaled. Unhappiness simmered between them. Broad shoulders flexing, he said, "Normally, I'd be happy to do that—"

And here they went. "Let me guess," she scoffed. "You don't have time for that?"

Another grimace. "Actually, no, I—we—likely don't."

"Well, that makes two of us," Tess huffed, figuring this conversation had come to an end. "Now, if you will excuse me…" Hoping he'd finally get the hint, she turned back to the front door of the Craftsman bungalow, slid the key into the lock, turned it and heard it open with a satisfying click.

Aware that Noah Lockhart was still standing behind her, despite the fact he had been summarily dismissed, she pushed the door open. Head held high, she marched across the threshold. And strode face-first into the biggest, stickiest spiderweb she had ever encountered in her life!

At the same time, she felt something gross and scary drop onto the top of her head. "Aggghhh!" she screamed, dropping her bag and backing up, frantically batting away whatever it was crawling through her thick, curly hair…

This, Noah thought ruefully, was exactly what Tess Gardner's new boss had feared. Sara Anderson McCabe had worried if Tess had seen the interior of the house she had inherited from her late uncle, before she toured the clinic and met the staff she was going to be working with, she might change her mind and head right back to Denver and the fancy veterinary practice she had come from.

Not that anyone had expected her to crash head-first into a spiderweb worthy of a horror movie.

He covered the distance between them in two swift steps, reaching her just as she backed perilously toward the edge of the porch, still screaming and batting at her hair. With good reason. The large, gray spider was still moving across her scalp, crawling from her crown toward her face.

Noah grabbed Tess protectively by the shoulders with one hand, and used his other to flick the pest away.

It landed on the porch and scurried into the bushes while Tess continued to shudder violently.

"You're okay," he told her soothingly, able to feel her shaking through the thick layer of her winter jacket. She smelled good, too, her perfume a mix of citrus and patchouli. "I got it off of you."

She sagged in relief. And reluctantly, he let her go, watching as she brushed at the soft cashmere sweater clinging to her midriff, then slid her hand down her jean-clad legs, grimacing every time she encountered more of the sticky web.

Damn, she was beautiful, with long, wildly curly blond hair and long-lashed, sage-green eyes. Around five foot eight, to his own six foot three inches, she was the perfect weight for her slender frame, with curves in all the right places, and she had the face of an angel.

Not that she seemed to realize just how incredibly beguiling she was. It was a fact that probably drove all the guys, including him, crazy.

Oblivious to the ardent nature of his thoughts, she shot him a sidelong glance. Took another deep breath. Straightened. "Was it a spider?"

Noah had never been one to push his way into

anyone else's business, but glad he had been there to help her out, he said, "Yes."

Her pretty eyes narrowed. "A brown recluse or black widow?"

He shook his head. "A wolf spider."

"Pregnant with about a million babies?"

He chuckled. "Aren't they always?"

She muttered something beneath her breath that he was pretty sure wasn't in the least bit ladylike. Then, pointing at the ceiling several feet beyond the still open front door, where much of the web was still dangling precariously, she turned back to regard him suspiciously. "Did you know it was there? Is that why you told me not to go in alone?"

He held her gaze intently. He hadn't been this aware of a woman since he'd lost his wife, but there was something about Tess that captured—and held—his attention. A latent vulnerability, maybe. "It never would have occurred to me that was what you would have encountered when you opened the door."

Squinting, she propped her hands on her hips. "Then why the warning about not going in alone?"

Good question. Since he had never been known to chase after damsels in distress. Or offer help indiscriminately. He had always figured if someone wanted his aid, that person would let him know, and then he would render it in a very trustworthy fashion. Otherwise, he stayed out of it. Tonight, though, he hadn't. Which was…interesting…given how many problems of his own he had to manage.

She was still waiting for his answer.

He shrugged, focusing on the facts. "Waylon hadn't been here for at least a year, before he passed four months ago, and he was never known for his domestic skills." So he honestly hadn't known what she would be walking into.

She scanned the neat front yard. Although it was only a little past five o'clock in the afternoon, the sun was already setting in the wintry gray sky. "But the lawn and the exterior of the house are perfectly maintained!"

"The neighbors do that as a courtesy for him."

"But not the interior?" she persisted.

"Waylon didn't want to trouble folks, so he never gave anyone a key."

Tess turned her gaze to the shadowy interior. All the window blinds were closed. Because it was turning dusk, the inside of the home was getting darker by the minute. And the mangled cobweb was still dangling in the doorway.

Noah knew it was none of his business. That she was an adult, free to do as she chose. Yet, he had to offer the kind of help he knew he would want anyone in his family to receive, in a similar situation.

"Sure you want to stay here alone?" Noah asked.

Actually, now that she knew what she was facing, Tess most definitely did *not* want to stay here tonight. "I don't have a choice," she admitted with grim resignation. "I don't have a hotel room. Everything in the vicinity is booked. I guess I waited too long to make a reservation."

He nodded, seemingly not surprised.

"The Lake Laramie Lodge and the Laramie Inn are always booked well in advance. During the week, it's business conferences and company retreats."

"And the weekends?" she queried.

"On Saturdays and Sundays it tends to be filled with guests in town for a wedding or family reunion, or hobby aficionados of some sort. This weekend I think there's a ham-radio conference... Next week, scrapbooking, maybe? You can look it up online or just read the signs posted around town, if you want to learn more."

"Good to know. Anyway..." Tess pulled her cell phone from her pocket and punched the flashlight button. Bright light poured out. "I'm sure I can handle it. Especially if we turn on the lights..."

She reached for the switches just inside the door. To her surprise, neither brought any illumination.

Noah glanced at the fixture on the ceiling inside the house, then the porch light. "Maybe the bulbs are just burned out," he said.

Stepping past the dangling web, he went on inside, to a table lamp. She watched as he tried it. Nothing.

Still wary of being attacked by another spider, she lingered just inside the portal, her hands shoved inside the pockets of her winter jacket. The air coming out of the interior of the house seemed even colder than the below-freezing temperature outside. Which meant the furnace wasn't on, either. Although that could be fixed.

Noah went to another lamp. Again, nothing happened when he turned the switch. "You think all the bulbs could be burned out?" Tess asked hopefully, knowing that at least that would be an easy fix.

"Or…" He strode through the main room to the kitchen, which was located at the rear of the two-story brick home. She followed him, careful to avoid plowing through another web, then watched as he pushed down the lever on the toaster. Peering inside the small appliance, he frowned.

Anxiety swirled through Tess, as she wondered what she had gotten herself into. "Not working, either?"

"No." Noah moved purposefully over to the sink and tried the faucet. When no water came out, he hunkered down and looked inside the cabinet below. Tried something else, but to no avail. As he straightened, three small mice scampered out, running past him, then disappeared behind the pantry door. Tess managed not to shriek while he grimaced, and concluded, "Both the electricity and water are turned off."

Which meant the mice and the spiders weren't the worst of her problems. "You're *kidding*!" After rushing to join him at the sink, she tried the ancient faucet herself. Again…nothing.

Noah reached for the cords next to the window above the sink and opened the dark wooden blinds. They were covered with a thick film of dust. As was, Tess noted in discouragement, everything else in sight.

Plus, the spiders had had a field day.

There were big cobwebs in every corner, stretched across the ceiling and the tops of the window blinds, and strewn over the beat-up furniture. Worse, when she looked closely, she could see mice droppings trailing across much of the floor. Which could mean she had more than the three rodent guests she had already encountered. *Ugh.*

"Seen enough for right now?" Noah asked.

Tess shook her head in dismay. She'd had such dreams for this place. Hoped it would give her the kind of permanent home and sense of belonging she had always yearned for. But while she was certainly taken aback by what they had discovered here tonight, she wasn't going to let it scare her off. Besides, in addition to the property, her late uncle had left her the proceeds of his life-insurance policy, with the expectation she would use the funds to fix up the house. "Maybe the upstairs will be better…"

Unfortunately, it wasn't. The single bathroom looked as if it hadn't had a good scrubbing in years. Two of the bedrooms were filled with piles of fishing and camping equipment. The third held a sagging bed, and heaps of clothes suitable for an oil roughneck who spent most of his time on ocean rigs.

On a whim, she checked out the light switch, and the sink in the bathroom, too. Neither worked.

Noah was gazing at her from a short distance away. "Well, that settles it, you can't stay here," he said.

Tess had already come to the same conclusion.

Although, after two very long days in her SUV,

she wasn't looking forward to the two-hour drive to San Antonio for an available hotel room.

He met her gaze equably. "You can come home with me."

Chapter Two

Noah may as well have suggested they run away together, given the astonished look on Tess Gardner's
pretty face. Then, without another word, she brushed
by him and headed down the staircase, still using her
cell-phone flashlight to lead the way.

Noah followed, giving her plenty of space. He had
an idea what she was feeling. He had been orphaned
as a kid and had lived in three different foster homes,
over a two-year period, before finally being reunited
with his seven siblings and adopted by Robert and
Carol Lockhart. So he knew firsthand what it was
like to be alone, in unfamiliar circumstances, with
those around you offering help you weren't sure it
was safe to take.

If he wanted to help her, and he did, he would have
to make sure she knew his intentions were honorable.

Being careful to avoid cobwebs, she walked out of the numbing cold inside the house, and onto the front porch, breathing deeply of the brisk air. Slender shoulders squared, she swung back to him. "Why would you want to do that for me?"

It wasn't lost on him that for a fiercely independent woman like her, an offer like this probably wasn't the norm. But for someone like him—who had finished growing up here—it was. Patiently, he explained, "Because this is Laramie County, and neighbors help neighbors out here all the time. Plus—" he winked, teasing, as if this was his only motive "—maybe it will give me an in with the new vet. But if you want, you could always call Sara Anderson McCabe—" their only mutual acquaintance, that he knew of, anyway "—for a character reference."

The mention of the other Laramie County veterinarian had Tess relaxing slightly. "First, I already did FaceTime with her earlier today. Both her kids are sick with strep throat. And on top of that, between the construction for the new addition on her house, the extra work at the veterinary clinic since the founding partner retired five weeks ago and the fact she is seven months pregnant, she is completely wiped out. I'm not about to add anything to her already full slate."

Noah admired Tess's compassion. That she was willing and able to put others first, even when her own situation was far less than ideal, spoke volumes about this newcomer. Perhaps Sara had been right. Even though the two of them had kind of gotten off on the wrong foot, his gut told him that Tess was going to fit right into this rural community.

She studied him even more closely, then after a pause, admitted wearily, "And second, it's not necessary. I already know what Sara's going to say when it comes to your character. Since you were first on the list of eligible men she thought I should meet."

Noah frowned. His old friend had already been matchmaking? This was news to him. But perhaps not such an unexpected occurrence for the gorgeous woman standing opposite him.

He studied the guileless look in Tess's light green eyes.

"Initially, I sort of assumed that was why you were here," she continued dryly, with a provoking lift of her brow. "To get a jump on the competition?"

Glad to know he wasn't the only one who routinely tried to find the irony or humor in every situation, Noah stifled his embarrassment and scrubbed a hand over his face.

As long as they were going to talk candidly...

He met her casually probing gaze. "Ah, no." Romance had most definitely *not* been on his mind when he had stopped by the house on a whim, to see if she had arrived or if there was anything he could do for the town's newest resident. "Since my wife passed a couple of years ago, I've had my hands full with my three little girls. And I don't see that changing anytime soon."

Her eyes widening in obvious surprise, she stepped toward him. Up and down the block, the time-activated streetlamps suddenly switched on, spreading yellow light through the increasing winter gloom and enabling her to peer at him even more closely. She tilted her head up to his. "So, you're *not* interested in dating?"

He shook his head. A woman like this...well, she could make him forget his new, more cautious approach to life. And that was something he just couldn't risk.

She sighed in obvious relief and stepped back.

He watched the color come into her high, sculpted cheeks. "And you?" Noah asked.

"No," she said emphatically. "I'm definitely not on the market."

Their eyes locked.

"Although I am interested in meeting new people..." she said, then paused. "Making friends," she added eventually.

Noah exhaled. "Can never have enough of those," he said, meaning it. It was his friends and family who had helped him through the past few tumultuous years.

And would continue to help him.

Because as rough as it had been to weather the emotional impact of losing the first and only love of his life, it was even harder to face life as a single dad.

"So about that offer to bunk at your place tonight..." Tess said, pacing the length of the porch, squinting to evaluate. "It really wouldn't be an inconvenience?"

Wanting to give her the kind of small-town Texas welcome his friends Sara and Matt McCabe had wanted for her, Noah shook his head. "Nah. I've got a big house with a nice guest suite. But if you get there and you're not comfortable with the setup for any reason, you could always take refuge at my folks' ranch house just down the road. They are babysitting my three girls this evening, so you'll have a chance to meet them, too." He released a breath. "And if you're *still* not comfortable with that option, my mom is a social worker for Laramie County, so it's possible she might be able to pull some strings and find you a place to bunk for the night."

Tess pursed her lips. "Like where?"

"Uh… I honestly don't know," he admitted. "Maybe there's an on-call room at the hospital that's not being used?"

She ran a hand through her thick mane of curly hair. "This is getting ridiculously complicated."

"You're right. And it doesn't have to be. So what do you say?" he asked her gruffly. "How about you lock up here, and we head out to my place?"

When she still looked a little hesitant, he added, "You can follow in your Tahoe. Check out the accommodations. And we can take it from there."

Fortunately, the drive was an easy one. And fifteen minutes later, Noah was turning his charcoal-gray Expedition onto a paved driveway off the country road they'd been traveling on, winding his way past the mailbox. Tess was right behind him, in her red SUV.

The black wrought-iron archway over the entrance

proclaimed the property to be the Welcome Ranch. Which was ironically appropriate, given the circumstances, Tess couldn't help but think.

Neat fences surrounded the manicured property. In the distance, a sprawling home could be seen. The impressive two-story abode featured California architecture, with an ivory stucco exterior. There were plenty of windows, and the first floor was all lit up. In the distance she could also see a grassy paddock and a big, elegant barn that looked as if it had been recently built.

She didn't notice any livestock grazing in the moonlit pastures. But she supposed there could be horses stabled in the barn.

Noah parked next to an extended-cab pickup that was in front of the four-car garage. Tess took the space next to that. As they got out, the front door opened, and a handsome couple in their midfifties stepped out and stood beneath the shelter of the portico.

He fell into step beside her. "My folks," he explained as he ushered her toward them. "Mom, Dad, this is Tess Gardner, the new veterinarian at the Laramie clinic. Tess, my parents, Robert and Carol Lockhart."

"Oh, you're here to see Miss Coco!" Carol Lockhart exclaimed, making an incorrect assumption. A slender woman with short dark hair and vivid green eyes, she was dressed in a cashmere turtleneck, tailored wool slacks and comfortable-looking winter boots.

Her tall, dark-haired husband had the year-round tan and fit appearance of someone who spent his life working outdoors. He nodded at Tess in approval. "Mighty nice of you."

Noah shifted closer to Tess and lifted a halting palm, before any further assumptions could be made. "That's not happening tonight," he said definitively, looking chagrined at the way his parents were jumping to conclusions. "Tess isn't starting work at the clinic until Monday, and she has had a really long day. Or actually, probably a couple of very long days."

He was right about that. Tess's muscles ached from the two-day, 800-plus-mile drive from Denver to Laramie County. Some of it over mountain roads. Much of it in inclement weather. Still, she didn't want anyone making decisions about what she was or wasn't up to. Curious, she turned back to his mother. "Who is Miss Coco?"

Carol explained, "Noah and the girls' miniature donkey. Noah's been worrying nonstop about her the last few weeks. So when he heard you had cared for a lot of mules back in Colorado during your fellowship, and were considered quite the expert, he was ecstatic."

Noah exhaled. He sent his mother a look that said he did not appreciate Carol speaking for him. "I wouldn't say ecstatic, exactly."

"Relieved, maybe?" his dad suggested.

"Something like that," Noah murmured.

Frowning in confusion, his mom turned back to

him. "So if Tess isn't here to see Miss Coco tonight, then...?"

"I'm afraid I didn't plan my arrival very well," Tess admitted, chagrined. "I thought the house I inherited from my uncle would be clean and empty. It was neither. There's also no electricity or water."

Noah added matter-of-factly, "Unfortunately, as you know, the offices that can turn the utilities back on won't be open until Monday. All the lodging in the area is booked. So I offered to let her bunk here temporarily."

Carol and Robert both smiled, understanding. Before they could say anything else, he asked, "Were the girls well-behaved for you?"

His parents nodded. "They went to bed at eight o'clock and went right to sleep," his dad said.

The interior of the house did seem quiet.

A lethargic chocolate-brown Labrador retriever ambled out on the porch. Recognizing an animal lover when he saw one, he went straight for Tess. She kneeled to greet him, letting him sniff her while she scratched him behind the ears. With a blissful huff, he sat down next to her, leaning his body against her legs.

"You know...we could stay a few more minutes if you all want to walk out to the barn, just for a minute," Carol suggested hopefully.

Tess had the idea that the older woman was worried about the miniature donkey, too. Although no one had yet said exactly why...

Her fatigue fading, the way it always did when

there was an animal in need of care, she turned back to Noah. A little embarrassed she hadn't been more helpful when he had tried to talk to her earlier, she asked, "Is that where Miss Coco is housed?"

Noah nodded.

"We could stay with the girls until you're back from the barn," Carol offered. "And I know Noah would feel better if you just took a quick peek at Miss Coco."

So would Tess. Appreciating the unexpectedly warm welcome from both Noah and his folks, she smiled. "Just let me get my medical bag out of my SUV."

"You really don't have to do this," Noah said as they took off across the lawn, toward a big slate-gray barn that looked as new as the house.

He paused to slide open the door and turn on the overhead lighting. The floor was concrete and there were a half-dozen stalls made of beautiful wood, and a heater was circulating warm air. He motioned for her to come inside.

Aware how comfortable she already felt with him, Tess smiled. "The least I can do, given how truly hospitable you have been."

Their eyes met. With a brief businesslike nod in her direction, he pulled the door shut, to keep in the heat, and led the way forward.

Tess had to quicken her steps to keep up with him. As she neared him, she caught another whiff of his woodsy scent, and something else, maybe the soap or shampoo he used, that was brisk and masculine.

A tingle of awareness surged through her. She pushed it away. She had mixed work and pleasure once, to a heartbreaking result. She couldn't allow herself to react similarly here. Especially to a man whose heart was ultimately as closed off as her ex's had been. "So what has you so concerned?" She forced herself to get back to business. "Can you give me a little history…?"

He paused and placed one hand over the top of the middle stall on the right. "Eight months ago, I went to the local 4-H adoption fair with my oldest daughter, Lucy." He eased open the stall door, gazing tenderly down at the miniature jennet curled up sleepily on fresh hay. "She fell in love with Miss Coco the minute she saw her…"

Tess gazed down at her new patient, entranced. "I can see why. Oh, Noah. She is beautiful!" With a light brown coat the color of powdered cocoa, a white stripe that went from her ears down her face, to the base of her throat, and white socks and tail, Tess figured the miniature donkey measured about two and a half feet tall. Her eyes were big and dark, and she was watching them carefully.

"Luckily, she has a personality to match. The problem is, I didn't know she was gestating when we adopted her. I just assumed her belly was a little swollen from lack of care. By the time I found out it wasn't an issue of malnutrition or lack of exercise, Lucy—my oldest—was already very attached."

Tess kneeled next to Coco, petting her. "And you don't want two donkeys." She opened up her bag.

"It's not really that. As you can see, I obviously have space for them. It's my three-year-old twins I am worried about. Lucy's eight. She can follow directions and understands there is no negotiation when it comes to the safety and welfare of animals in our care. The rules are the rules. Period."

Tess examined Coco's belly and the area around the birth canal, finding everything just as it should be. She reached for her stethoscope, pausing to listen to the strong, steady beat of Coco's heart, the breath going in and out of her lungs. Then she listened to the foal nestled inside. All was great.

She removed the earbuds and turned back to Noah. "And the twins…?"

"Are still at an excitable age. Angelica is sweet and mellow most of the time. A follower. Avery, on the other hand, has a real mind of her own. When she sets out on a mission, whatever it is, it can be hard to rein her in."

Tess laid the stethoscope around her neck and resumed petting Coco. She gazed up at Noah, who was still standing with his back to the side of the stall, the edges of his jacket open, his arms folded in front of him. He had the kind of take-charge, yet inherently kind, aura she admired. And if she were emotionally available, she'd be a goner. "Are you worried the twins will be too rough with the foal and that the baby's mama might be too protective and hurt them?"

He nodded with no hesitation. "Both—if the twins get too wound up. But I heard about something called imprint training, where you teach an animal from the moment they are born to trust and love the human touch. Which really gentles them. Sara said you gave classes in it, back in Colorado."

The ambient lighting in the stable made him look even more handsome. Which was definitely some-thing she did not need to be noticing. Any more than how good he smelled. Or how strong and fit his body looked in business-casual clothing.

Fighting the shiver of sensual awareness sliding through her, she forced herself to smile back at him. "I did."

His gaze sifted over her, igniting tiny sparks of electricity everywhere he looked. "And you plan to give them here?"

Tess nodded. "When I get settled in, yes."

His expression fell in disappointment.

"But I could help show you what to do, in the meantime, so you will be prepared."

He cocked an eyebrow, his good humor return-ing. "Private lessons?"

One lesson, maybe. Ignoring the potent masculinity and charisma radiating from him, she returned dryly, "I don't think it will take you all that long to get the hang of what to do. In the meantime, Miss Coco and her baby are doing fine. Everything is as it should be."

"Any idea when she will go into labor and deliver?" he asked, concerned.

She studied the conflicted expression on his face. "I'm guessing you heard that a miniature jennet's gestation period can last anywhere from eleven to fourteen months."

He nodded.

"Right now, I'm guessing it will be another one to two weeks." Tess put her stethoscope back in her vet bag and closed the clasp. She rose to her feet. When her shearling lined boots unexpectedly slid a little on the crushed hay, Noah put out a hand to steady her, the warmth of his hand encircling her wrist. His gentle, protective touch sent another storm of sensations through her. She worked to hold back a flush.

Gallantly, he waited until he was sure she had her footing, then let her go slowly. He stepped back, folding his arms across his chest once again. The warmth inside her surged even more as he looked her in the eye. "How will I know when it's time?" he asked.

She replied in the same serious tone. "A number of things will happen. The foal will turn and move into the birth canal. Miss Coco'll be restless and may even look thinner. And she'll be holding her tail away from her body to one side. At that point, she will need to be closely monitored twenty-four seven."

Noah began to look overwhelmed again.

Together, they walked out. "What about being here when Miss Coco's foal is born?" He paused just outside the barn doors. "Will you do that for us, to make sure everything goes all right?"

Tess nodded. "Be happy to," she promised with a reassuring smile. Ushering new life into the world was the best part of her job.

As they reached the porch, the fatigue hit her, hard. Noah went to get her two bags out of her Tahoe, while Carol showed her where to wash up and poured her a hot cup of tea. By the time he'd returned, his parents were already half out the door.

He regarded her sympathetically. "What else can I get you?"

Her hands gripping the mug, Tess shook her head. "Nothing. Thanks. All I want is a hot shower, and a bed. Time to sleep."

He gave her an understanding look. "I'll show you the guest suite."

She followed Noah as he led the way up the stairs, then past two rooms, where his three daughters could be seen snuggled cozily in their beds, sleeping in the glow of their night-lights.

Tess couldn't help but think how lucky he was, to have such a beautiful family and nice home, as the two of them moved silently past his girls, to the very end of the hall.

Oblivious to her quiet envy, he showed her the nicely outfitted guest suite with a private bath, chaise lounge just right for reading and comfortable-looking queen-size bed. He set her bags down just inside the door, in full host mode. "If there is anything you need that's not in the bathroom, let me know." He stepped back into the hall, and as their eyes met, a new warmth spiraled through her. He continued in a low, husky voice calibrated not to wake his daughters. "The kitchen is fully stocked, so make yourself at home there, too."

"Thank you," Tess returned, just as softly, marveling at his kindness, even as she reminded herself he had already stated that, just like her, he was not emotionally available. For anything more than a casual friendship, anyway. "I will."

"Well…" He cleared his throat, suddenly looking as reluctant to part company as she was. Which made her wonder if the latent physical attraction went both ways.

Giving no clue as to what he was thinking, he nodded at her. "See you in the morning."

A distracting shiver swept through her once again.

Working to slow her racing pulse, she responded with an inner casualness she couldn't begin to feel. "Sure, see you then." She smiled as he turned to walk away. And just like that, she was on her own for the rest of the night.

Chapter Three

Hours later, Noah was awakened from a deep sleep. "Daddy, there was a pretty lady in the kitchen, and she said to give you this when you waked up," Lucy said importantly. She and her twin sisters climbed onto his bed, the twins on one side, Lucy perched on the other.

Damn. He'd overslept. Noah scrubbed a hand over his face. *Not exactly the way he wanted to start the day.*

"Are you awake now?" Avery asked. "'Cause we want to know what the letter says. And Lucy still has trouble reading cursive."

"Okay." Noah sat up. A piece of paper was pushed into his hand. "'Noah,'" he began, reading out loud. "'Thanks so much for all your help and hospitality last night. Tess Gardner.'"

Nothing about seeing each other again.

Noah felt a wave of disappointment move through him. He couldn't say why exactly, but he had expected a little more. Something warmer or more personal. But then, she'd said she wasn't looking for anything more than friendship. Same as him. And she did have a lot on her slate.

A lot of which she was still going to need help with.

He thought about the look on her face when she'd run into that giant spiderweb, how it had felt to step in to rescue her, and feel her brush up against him, for one long incredible moment. He swallowed, pushing aside another wave of unexpected yearning.

He hadn't been close to anyone since Shelby had died. Hadn't wanted to be. Initially, it had been because he was still grieving and couldn't imagine anyone ever taking her place. Later, because he didn't want to risk the pain that came with a loss like that. He'd also known he hadn't the time or energy to try and incorporate someone special into his life. Never mind worry about how his girls would react if he did ever start dating again. So to feel fiercely attracted to Tess now was…well, unexpected, at the very least.

Feeling like the worst host ever, he swallowed. "Did she leave?" *Please tell me she hasn't gone yet.*

"Uh-huh. But she said to tell you that she looked in on Miss Coco and she's fine this morning, too. And also she took Tank out to the barn with her, so he probably won't need to go out for a while, although he will need to be fed. She gave him fresh water."

Pleased by the unexpected help, he smiled, ruminating softly. "That was nice of her..."

"Who is *she*?" Lucy queried, looking protective. She flung her long, tangly hair out of her eyes. Hair she did not brush nearly enough. Unlike her twin sisters, who were always brushing and styling each other's hair. "And why was she in *our house*? And why didn't we ever see her before this morning?"

Unable to get out of bed with the girls perched on either side of him, and unwilling to make them move just yet, Noah pushed up, so he was sitting against the headboard. He figured this was as good a time as any to have this conversation. "The nice lady's Dr. Tess Gardner. The new veterinarian I was telling you girls about. The one who knows a whole lot about taking care of miniature donkeys and their foals. She just moved here yesterday, and she came by last night to check out Miss Coco for us." At least that was what had ended up happening. Which was a good thing. It had given them a chance to get to know each other a little better, and see each other in a different light.

As he had watched Tess care for their miniature donkeys, it was easy to see why Sara had been so determined to get Tess to accept a position at the vet clinic in town. Tess was a very skilled clinician. Gentle. Thorough. Kind. And professional.

All were traits he considered essential.

In a veterinarian.

In a friend...

And of course she was very beautiful, and sexy in that breezy girl-next-door way, too.

Not that he should be noticing…

Exhaling, Noah continued, "Dr. Tess checked on Miss Coco's baby foal, too. And it was all good. Both were healthy as could be."

His three daughters readily accepted his explanation, for why Tess had been in their kitchen so early in the morning.

Although, Lucy gave it more thought, and her eyes widened. "She watched over Miss Coco *all night*? In the stable?"

Noah shook his head. "She slept in the house."

"Why?" Lucy's scowl deepened.

Patiently, Noah explained, "There was an unexpected mess-up with Dr. Tess's plans. Her house didn't have any power or water. The hotels were full, and she needed a place to sleep, so I offered her our guest room."

His eight-year-old folded her arms in front of her, and her lower lip slid out, into a pout. "Only our grandma and grandpa sleep in the guest room," she reminded him archly. "Or our aunts and uncles."

"Well, last night it was Dr. Tess."

Lucy continued to mull over that fact, not necessarily happily. Since all seven of his siblings had found love and gotten married recently, she had made it clear on numerous occasions that she was worried he would do the same. While she liked the attention of adult women, and the feminine, maternal perspective they brought, she didn't want anyone taking her late mother's place.

Initially, he hadn't, either.

But lately...seeing the rest of his family all paired up and so happy, he had begun to realize just how lonely he was. Having kids was great.

It was even better when you had someone to share them with.

But the woman who took his late wife's place in their lives was not going to be just anyone.

She'd have to be full of life and love. Independent. Kind. Giving.

Sort of like... Tess Gardner. Hold on! Where in the hell had *that* thought come from?

Lucy was frowning. "Hmm."

Figuring a change of subject was in order, Noah motioned for the girls to move. As soon as they hopped off the bed, he threw back the covers and swung his legs over the edge. "Who wants to go with me to give Tank his breakfast and then run down to the barn and check on Miss Coco?"

"Me!" all three girls squealed in unison.

"Then get your barn boots on," he said, shoving aside all thoughts of Tess and the impact she'd had on him in only a few glorious hours. "And I'll meet you in the kitchen."

"Well, what do you think?" Sara Anderson Mc-Cabe asked, after she had shown Tess around the veterinary clinic, and introduced her to all the staff before weekend office hours started at nine o'clock on Saturday morning.

The effervescent managing partner walked Tess into the small room with a desk that would serve as Tess's private office. With its polished linoleum floor, and standard office desk and chair, it was nothing like the luxurious office at her job in Denver. Yet, somehow, it was so much warmer.

"Are you going to be able to be happy here?" Sara asked, squinting at her.

Tess nodded. "I'm sure I will be." Everyone was just so darn nice. Including, and especially, Noah Lockhart. Not that she should be thinking of him...

Sara rested her palm on her pregnant belly. "Did you find a hotel to stay in until the movers get your belongings here from Denver? Or were you going to just go ahead and move into the house you inherited, as is?"

"Well, there was a slight problem with that." Briefly, she explained about the lack of utilities, and abundance of spiders and mice.

"Oh, no."

Oh, *yes*...

Sara shook her head, not looking all that surprised, now that she'd had a moment to think about it. "Well, Waylon wasn't known for his housekeeping. Not that he was ever home for long. When he came in off the oil rigs, all he ever wanted to do was go fishing until it was time to head back to the Gulf." She sighed. "But I had no idea he turned all his home's utilities off during his absences. Although I suppose it makes sense. Financially, anyway." She gave Tess another thoughtful squint. "So what did you do?"

"Um…"

This was a rural county. Sara was bound to find out, anyway. Not that it had been a secret.

Tess swallowed. "Noah Lockhart offered to put me up last night, at the Welcome Ranch."

Sara did a double take, unable to completely contain her pleased look. "You met Noah?"

"Yeah. He stopped by while I was looking at my uncle Waylon's house." *And gallantly saved me from more than a few spiders.*

The woman's eyes lit up hopefully. "What did you think?"

That she had never met anyone who could take her breath away with just a look, the way he could.

Aware Sara was still waiting for her reaction, Tess shook her head, struggling for something she *could* say. Finally, she sobered and managed a response. "He's, um, very tall." About six foot three inches to her own five foot eight. *And handsome.* "And, uh, helpful." Oh, Lord, what was this? When had she ever been so tongue-tied? Or felt like such a teenager? One with a secret crush?

Sara laughed. She lifted a halting palm. "Okay, I won't pry. Moving on. So what's your plan now?"

That was the problem. Tess didn't really have one. Yet. "Well, I can't get the power and water turned on until their offices open on Monday. But I have an exterminator meeting me at the house this afternoon. And I'm going to spend the rest of the day just getting my bearings and figuring out what I need."

Concern radiated from Sara. "Do you have a place to stay in the meantime?"

Tess nodded. "I made a reservation at a River Walk hotel in San Antonio for the next two nights." Although she was hoping not to need to drive all that way if she could get her new home clean enough to camp out in for the next few days.

"Somewhere with spa services, I hope?" the other woman teased.

Tess chuckled in response, then grabbed her purse and keys. "Anyway, I better get going."

Sara walked her as far as the employees' entrance. "Let me know if you do need anything. Including a place to stay. Matt and the kids and I can always make room."

Tess knew that. She just didn't like depending on others for anything. It was always much better when she could handle things on her own. Which was exactly what she planned to do.

Several hours later, Tess had everything she needed for the cleanup of her new home to begin. She headed for Spring Street. No sooner had she parked, than a now-familiar charcoal-gray Expedition pulled up behind her.

Noah stepped out.

Unlike the evening before, when he'd been garbed in business-casual, he was dressed in a pair of old jeans and a flannel shirt, as well as a thick fleece vest and construction-style work boots.

He looked so good he made her mouth water.

Pushing away the unwanted desire, she met him at the tailgate of her Tahoe. Despite herself, she was glad he had come to her rescue again. She tilted her head back to look into his eyes. "Seriously, cowboy, we have to stop meeting like this."

He grinned at her droll tone. His midnight blue eyes took on the sexy glint she was beginning to know so well. "I figured you were going to need help."

He had figured right. What she hadn't decided was if it was a good idea or a bad idea to allow herself to depend on him. Especially because she had been down this road before, only to have it end disastrously.

Pushing all thoughts of her ex and their failed relationship away, she opened up her tailgate. Determined now to focus on the gargantuan task at hand.

He saw the big box. "A wet-dry vac. Good idea."

His approval warmed her. Why, she didn't know. She inhaled the masculine scent of his soap and shampoo. "It will be when I finally get electricity on Monday."

At least she *hoped* it would be on Monday.

Out here in the country, there was no guarantee they offered same-day service, for an extra fee, the way they did in the city.

Grateful for his lack of recrimination or judgment, with regard to her lack of proper planning, Tess let

Noah help her slide the bulky box onto the ground. He smiled genially, as relaxed as she was stressed.

Nonsensically, she chattered on. "I figured it was the fastest way to get up all the crud inside and dispose of it."

He scanned her work clothes and equally no-nonsense boots. Her own quarter-zip fleece jacket.

"In the meantime," she sighed, lifting out the rest of her purchases, "there's the old-fashioned way, of broom, dustpan and trash bag."

Noah stepped closer, inundating her with the heat and strength of his big masculine body. Then he rubbed his hand across his closely shaven jaw, before dropping it once again. "Actually—" he let his gaze drift over her face before returning to her eyes "—we could use your shop vac today. If you don't mind borrowing some electrical power from a neighbor."

He really knew how to tempt her. But... "I can't ask someone I don't know."

He chuckled, a deep rumbling low in his throat. "Sure, you can," he drawled, surveying her as if he found her completely irresistible. Another shimmer of tension floated between them and she felt her breath catch in her throat. What was it about this man that drove her to distraction? "Neighbors help each other out around here. Remember? But I can understand your reluctance to ask for a favor, when you meet the new neighbors for the first time. So if you want—" he placed a reassuring hand on her shoulder, the warmth of his touch emanating through her clothes "—I can rustle up some outdoor extension cords, go next door and set that up for you. As well as help you put the wet-dry vac together."

The part of her that wanted to keep her heart under lock and key responded with a resounding *No!* The temptation to lean on Noah Lockhart was too strong as it was. But the more practical part of her felt differently. She had to be at work at her new job, seeing patients, forty-eight hours from now. And right now, like it or not, the house she had inherited was definitely not livable.

She drew in a deep, enervating breath and dared to meet his eyes, trying not to think how attracted she was to him. She swallowed hard. "Sure." She forced herself to sound casual. As if she was used to such random kindness in her life. She took out the rest of the cleaning products and microfiber cloths, and shut the SUV tailgate. "Thanks... I would really appreciate that."

He picked up the bulky box and easily carried it up the front steps to the porch. "Now we're talking."

She followed with the bags. When they were face-to-face again, she tilted her head at him, curious. "Not that I'm not grateful for the help, but don't you have responsibilities of your own to tend to?"

He came near enough that she could feel his hot breath fanning against her skin. "My girls are on a play date with their cousins, over at my parents' ranch."

He whipped out his cell phone, punched a button on the screen and began typing. To whom, she didn't know.

"I'm supposed to join them at six this evening, for dinner," he explained.

But until then, the implication was, he was free to do whatever he felt like doing.

"Nice." She set down her things, then fished around in the front pocket of her jeans for her keys. Unable to help herself, she added with an appreciative smile, "Your daughters were very cute, by the way."

The proud, affectionate look on Noah's face told her he knew he had hit the jackpot when it came to his kids. She could not help but agree.

Wistfully, once again, she wished she had a few of her own just like them. In fact, as far as timing went, she had thought she would be married, with at least one child by now. But she had fallen in love with someone who ultimately hadn't felt the same, so…

He finished texting. Glancing up, his eyes scanned her face, his expression serious now. "I hope they were polite to you this morning."

Tess reflected on the three pajama-clad little girls, with their pink cheeks and tousled hair. The three-year-old twins had their daddy's deep blue eyes. Their big sister, Lucy, was lovely, too. Albeit observant and intuitive. Guarded. Aware he was waiting on her reply, she said finally, "I think they were more shocked than anything."

He lifted an eyebrow. Urging…no, more like demanding that she go on.

Tess cleared her throat. "Lucy made it clear women

did not spend the night at the Welcome Ranch, unless they were family." *Which I am definitely not.*

"Ah, well…" He slid his phone into his pocket. "As I said, I'm not looking for a new woman in my life."

Which should be reassuring.

It had been yesterday.

Now, that knowledge just left her feeling off-kilter. The way she always did when she allowed herself to want something that was not likely to happen. Like she had with her ex. Thinking that time—and increasing intimacy—and a more settled lifestyle after the super demanding years of vet school and residency—would ease them into a blissful future. And give them both the lifelong commitment and family that she had yearned for.

Unfortunately, her ex had other ideas. And priorities.

Noah's phone tinged, signaling an incoming text. He pulled it out and looked at the screen. Smiled, as he announced, "My brother Gabe lives a few blocks over. He's got a few outdoor extension cords we can borrow. He's going to bring them right over."

Another pleasant surprise. She could so get used to this. "That's nice of him."

"Yeah."

Tess unlocked the front door and carefully led the way inside. It was as icy cold and musty-smelling as the day before. To the point that all she could think was *ugh*.

Eminently calm, Noah looked up. "The spiders were busy."

The cowboy standing beside her was right. New webs were everywhere. Tess sighed. She hoped this wasn't an omen. "They certainly were."

Chapter Four

"Want to take a break?" Noah asked, an hour later.

Looking even more overwhelmed than she had when they had first walked in, Tess nodded. She sighed, completely vulnerable now as she met his gaze, seeming on the verge of tears.

It was easy to see why she was so demoralized, Noah thought. While the exterior of the brick home was pristine, the interior of the house looked like something out of an episode of *Hoarders*. And though they had been knocking webs down from the ceiling and windows with the broom, and vacuuming up dirt and debris, there was still so much to do.

Tess shoved a hand through her wild butterscotch-blond curls. Her elegant features were tinged an emotional pink. He moved close enough to see the frustration glimmering in her eyes. "I mean it helps to have some of the dust and gunk gone," she said, flashing him a grateful half smile, "but I still kind of feel like all we're doing at the moment is rearranging the deck chairs on the *Titanic*."

"Yeah. I can see that analogy." He stepped nearer. It was all he could do not to take her in his arms and comfort her. But he knew that could lead to trouble with a capital *T*. "Do you think it would help if we cleared out a room or two? Just made some space?"

Her teeth raked her plump lower lip. "Probably, yeah." A look of relief flashed on her face.

Next question.

Savoring her nearness and the pleasure that came from being alone with her like this, he asked, "Is it going to be difficult for you to sort through this stuff?"

She shoved her hands in the pockets of her jeans. The take-charge veterinarian was back. "No. There are only two things I'm keeping. The first is that rusted-out cast-iron skillet in the kitchen that I'm pretty sure belonged to my grandmother. The second are the fishing lures my uncle made, and one of his tackle boxes to keep them in. Everything else that can be donated will be. The stuff that can't will be trashed."

He liked her decisiveness. "What is your timetable for getting this all done?"

Another shadow crossed her face. Their eyes locked, providing another wave of unbidden heat between them. "Ah, yesterday," she joked, running her hands through her hair again.

He noticed how the midday sunshine, which was flooding in through the grimy windows, caught the shimmer of gold in her blond hair.

He reached over and took her hand in his, wondering what it would take to make her feel as crazy with longing and giddy with desire as he did at this moment. "What would you say if I could make that happen?"

She peered at him, the corners of her luscious lips turning up slightly. *"Are you serious?"*

Pushing aside the primal urge to kiss her, he took a deep, calming breath and watched her retreat into scrupulous politeness. "Well, not the yesterday part. I haven't mastered time travel yet," he quipped, letting go of her hand and once again giving her the physical space she seemed to require. He curtailed his own rising emotions. "But I *could* probably get this place cleared out for you today."

"How?" She folded her arms against her middle, the action pushing up the soft curves of her breasts. "Do you have trash haulers and charity pickup on speed dial?"

He had been ready for this kind of reticence, given how high she had her guard up. "Close. Six of my seven siblings live in Laramie County. And the sister who doesn't is visiting with her husband and twins this weekend. So they're at my parents' ranch."

"Still—" another beleaguered sigh "—it's pretty last-moment."

He wondered what it would take to begin to tear down the walls around her heart. And allow his own to come tumbling down in the process. "Let me guess. You don't want to impose."

She winced, looking uncomfortable again. "I really don't."

He locked eyes with her. "How about this then? I'll send out a Lockhart family text, asking for volunteers. And we'll see what happens."

"Un-be-liev-able!" Tess said five hours later. She waved at the pest-control associate, who was backing out of her driveway. Then turned to Noah, unable to help but smile, as the two of them walked back inside the house. The rooms had been completely cleared out of all debris and swept clean. She went from room to room, amazed at how spacious the house seemed, now that the rooms were empty. "I can't believe this was done in just five hours!"

"I know." Noah glanced around appreciatively, too. "Isn't my family fantastic?"

"They certainly are." They'd started showing up minutes after he'd sent out his SOS text. His sister-in-law Allison, a lifestyle blogger, had instinctively known what could be repurposed and what could not. His brother-in-law Zach had brought his Callahan Custom Carpentry delivery truck. Others had pickups and SUVs. The women sorted stuff inside, and the men carried things out. All of them talking and joking, and warmly welcoming her to the community.

For the first time in her life, Tess had a glimpse of what it would be like to be part of a big, loving family. To have people you could count on to be there for you, even on short notice. Growing up the only child of a single mom, with her only other blood relatives—the uncle and grandmother she never really knew—in Texas, Tess'd had to learn to rely mostly on herself, and her mom, when her mom was around. After her mom had died, she'd had her ex. But since she and Carlton had split, she had only her casual friends, who were just as caught up in their busy lives, as she had been. To suddenly be surrounded by so many warm and generous people was a revelation.

And in Laramie County, Texas, apparently the norm.

Achingly aware of how cozy and enticing this all was, she took a seat next to him on the staircase steps. Somehow, they managed not to touch, but barely, given how big and manly Noah's tall frame was. They each held chilled bottles of water that had been donated by one of his sibs. "But you're not really surprised at the quick way they accomplished this, are you?"

He turned to her, his brawny shoulder nudging hers in the process. "They did the same for us, when the girls and I moved back from California, a few years ago. They had us all unpacked and everything organized and put away, in less than a day. So—" he shrugged amiably, pausing to take another long, deep drink "—I knew if we all worked together we could get it done. Even if my available siblings and or their spouses only came in for an hour or two each."

"Do they still help you, too?" Tess asked. Aware she had met all of his siblings except Mackenzie, who had been helping his mom with preparations for the family dinner scheduled for that evening.

"Yeah. We all help each other, although I think, at least for now," he frowned, "with me the only parent on scene for my three little girls, I'm doing more taking than giving." He exhaled, his expression turning more optimistic. "Although in time, I think that will change, and I'll be able to pay them back for all the help they give me, every week."

She studied his handsome profile. "What sort of things do they do?"

"My brothers help with any chore that requires more than one person—like putting up outside Christmas decorations or hauling hay for the barn. My sisters assist with clothes shopping. Which," he made a rueful face, "can be a hysterical mess if the girls think I don't understand what is pretty and what is not!" He tossed his head in mock, kid-drama.

She laughed at his comically indignant tone.

Having met his three girls, she could see each of them doing just that.

Resisting the urge to take his hand in hers, she prodded softly, "What else?"

"Oh. Well. They all carpool with me so I don't have to go into town twice daily on weekdays. My parents and sibs also take turns making an extra casserole or dinner, and drop one off with me, for our dinner. They have the girls over for sleepovers or playdates. Stuff like that."

"It sounds wonderful."

He nodded. "It is."

Feeling very glad he was there with her, despite herself, she got to her feet once again. Still tingling with awareness and something else—some other soul-deep yearning she chose not to identify—she began to pace. "Well, I'm going to have to figure out a way to thank them all."

He moved lazily to his feet. Tossed the empty bottle into the box earmarked for temporary recycling. Then, rocking forward on his toes, he hooked his thumbs into the loops on either side of his fly. "They don't expect anything in return except maybe a word of thanks, which you already said to each of them."

Tess knew that. She also knew she would feel better if she did more than that... But there was no time to figure that out now.

"So what's next?" Noah said.

It was five o'clock. Which reminded her... Tess dragged in a breath and retrieved her phone. "I need to cancel my hotel reservations in San Antonio." She pulled up the website and let them know she wouldn't be coming. "Done!"

He looked at her as if he could read her mind. Then quirked an eyebrow. "You're going to stay here tonight?"

Tess walked over to the fireplace and kneeled in front of it. She didn't have any wood, but she knew where the firewood-sales stand was. Her self-sufficient nature came back full-force. "That's the plan." She reached around for the handle that would open the flue. It seemed to be…stuck.

"Here. Let me." Noah kneeled beside her and easily managed what she had been unable to. The damper opened with a rusty screech.

Tess winced. "That doesn't sound good."

"No kidding." Still hunkered down on the hearth, he pulled out his phone, turned on the flashlight and aimed it up the chimney. A loud fluttering sound and several chirps followed. They both ducked in response. But fortunately, whatever bird, or *birds*, that had been there went up, not down into the house. Probably because the down exit had been blocked, and they likely assumed it still was.

"Come take a look," he said.

Curious, Tess leaned toward him and followed the beam of his light. "Oh, no. A nest." It looked as if the visitors had really made themselves at home for some time now.

"Yep." Noah aimed the beam across the interior walls. "And quite a bit of soot, too." He frowned in concern. "You're going to need to get a chimney sweep out here to clean it before you can safely build a fire in this."

Sitting back on her heels, Tess moaned and buried her face in her hands.

There went one of the most important parts of her plan.

He gave her a curious sidelong glance, and shut the flue. Moving smoothly to his feet, he chivalrously offered her a hand up.

Tess accepted his help, only because it would have been awkward not to, after all they had been through. Ignoring the sparks that started in her fingertips and spread outward through her entire body, she disengaged their grip, then took a big gulp of air. "Well, maybe I won't need to make a fire in there tonight," she mused, trying to look on the bright side, "if I can find a warm enough sleeping bag at the super store."

Somehow, he wasn't surprised to see her thinking about roughing it until she could get all the utilities turned on, and her belongings sent down from Denver.

"Or," he said, regarding her amiably, "you could stay with us again until your place is livable and all your stuff gets here."

He had no idea how tempting that idea sounded. Especially given the kindness of her host.

He winked at her playfully. "Unless the Welcome Ranch is too 'California' for your taste. And you need accommodations that are more Texan."

Tess rolled her eyes at his teasing. "You know it's not that," she drawled right back.

True, the style of his home was unexpected for this neck of the woods, where southwestern and Southern decor reigned. But it was beautiful and quite comfortable nevertheless.

She bit her lip and let out a long-suffering sigh. "I just don't want to impose."

"So—" he spread his hands wide "—we'll barter, to make things even. *You* check on Miss Coco and her foal, two times every day, until her little one is born and doing well. And the girls and I'll give you the shelter you need and all the privacy you want."

She chewed her lip, deliberating. The last thing she wanted was to be an imposition, and this arrangement he'd proposed was hardly a fair exchange. But there was no denying that it would be wonderful not to have to worry about making the house livable while simultaneously starting her new job.

Tess studied him intently, aware that they had known each other just twenty-four hours now and she already felt closer to him than most people she had known all her life. "You know, of course, that you are likely talking several weeks?" Which was a long time for a houseguest, especially one who was still a relative stranger.

He tilted his head, his seductive lips curving up in an inviting smile. "At least."

Oh, this could be trouble.

So much trouble, if she ever gave in to the attraction simmering between them and did something really crazy like kiss him…or let him kiss her.

And yet, with so few options, could she really afford to quibble? They were both adults, responsible ones at that. She could handle this. They both could.

"Well…?" he implored softly.

Her heartbeat kicked into high gear. "You really wouldn't mind?"

He sobered, then responded quietly, "I wouldn't offer if I did."

Silently, she went through all the rest of the reasons why and why not. Found, in the end, she was still leaning toward staying with him and his three adorable little girls. "And you really think that would be an even trade for several weeks of lodging…?"

He chuckled. "Given how nervous I am about birthing my first and probably only miniature donkey?" he said in a low, deadpan tone. "I sure as heck do."

She couldn't help but laugh at his comically feigned look of terror. She held up a palm. "Okay, I accept. But we do our own thing. You carry on as normal with your family and I will try not to get in the way."

He paused, as if trying to figure out how to phrase something. "That sounds fine," he said eventually. "In the meantime," he continued matter-of-factly, "you have been invited to my folks' ranch for dinner with the family. Most of whom you have already met."

The part of Tess who had become acquainted with most of his siblings and their spouses, and knew how nice they all were, wanted to accept the invitation. However, the other part of her, that needed to take a breath, knew what a bad idea it was.

She'd gotten romantically attached to a guy before, because she had found herself in a challenging situation and needed emotional support. Same as him.

While their relationship had continued through vet school, residency, and into their first jobs after graduation, their engagement had not ended well.

She had no intention of making the same mistake.

"Thank you, but I have a lot to do this evening.

Laundry and a few other chores…so if that's okay I'll pass on the offer." Then she realized she was being a little presumptuous. "But, um, if you'd rather I not use your washer and dryer, I saw a Laundromat in town. I could easily stop there…"

"Don't be silly. When I said make yourself at home, I meant it."

"Daddy, you are *not* being fair!"

Uh-oh, Tess thought as the shrill voice came her way.

Lucy stomped closer, bypassing the laundry room, where Tess had been working, through the back hallway, and into the kitchen, where she was now seated. Checking her email, on her laptop computer. "My bedtime is *always* a half hour later than the twins!"

"Under normal circumstances, yes," Noah returned calmly as he shut the back door behind them and ushered the weary-looking twins forward. He had a backpack slung over his shoulder, and a big foil-wrapped package in his hands that she guessed was dinner leftovers.

Avery and Angelica turned and gazed up. Their dad was so tall they had to tilt their heads way back to see his face. "Do we have to get a bath tonight?" Avery asked.

Noah set the platter on the kitchen island, then came back to the twins. "Do you want one?"

The three-year-olds looked at each other, deliberating. Avery stifled a yawn. "No. I just want to wash my face and brush my teeth and get in my pajamas."

"I want to do that, too," Angelica said, following her twin's lead.

Meanwhile, Lucy was storming the back hallway, her arms crossed in front of her. She was so worked up that steam was practically coming out of her ears.

Noah looked at Tess. "Sorry," he mouthed.

She gave him a smile and a nod, letting him know it was okay. Then watched as he pulled out a computer tablet from the *Family* backpack of all their stuff. "All right, Lucy, you can have twenty minutes of screen time. But then you're going upstairs and going to bed with no more argument. Understand?"

Rather than looking appeased, Lucy's sulky expression deepened. "Yes."

He pointed her in the direction of the great room. Sent another apologetic look at Tess and disappeared with the twins.

Trying not to imagine what it would be like to be part of a family like this, instead of coming home every day to a solitude that often seemed far too lonely, Tess returned to the laundry room. She continued pulling her clothes out of the dryer, then proceeded to deposit them in the wicker basket. She was just going to be here for a short while, she reminded herself. And she and Noah had agreed they would each do their own thing, without getting in each other's way. So there was no reason to offer to help him with anything. Except...

Lucy was back. Standing in the doorway. Tablet in her arms. In that moment, she looked very much like her take-charge daddy. "Aren't you coming?" she demanded.

Tess stood. She settled the basket on her hip, doing her best to exude the kind of casual tranquility she was pretty sure Lucy needed in this moment. "You want me to sit with you?" she asked as if it was no big deal. When it felt like a big deal to her. After all, what did she know about caring for kids?

"Well, duh."

"Um, sure." Making certain to give the child her space, Tess followed her to the big U-shaped sectional. She sat on one end. Still looking mighty unhappy, Lucy settled on the other, making no move to turn on her tablet.

Tess was surprised by the girl's attitude. She had been as welcoming as her two sisters, when they'd encountered her in the Welcome Ranch kitchen that morning. What had changed to make her resent Tess so? The fact that she was back? Intending to stay for a few weeks, at Noah's request? He had to have told them something. None of them had seemed shocked to see her there, sitting in front of her computer. Or doing her laundry.

Then again, maybe it's not about me. Maybe it has to do with someone or something else.

Tess favored Lucy with a gentle smile. "Did you have fun at the Circle L?"

She received another resentful scowl in return. Lucy peered at her suspiciously. "How do *you* know where we were?"

"Your dad told me."

Lucy got up and went over to a table in the foyer. She came back with two framed pictures. The first was a wedding photo of Noah and his late wife. Noah looked about a decade or so younger. His wife seemed to be about the same age. The other was of their family of five, when her mom had still been alive, and Lucy looked to have been around four or five, while the twins were still at the age where they weren't yet walking.

"This is my mommy," Lucy declared. "Her name is Shelby. She loved us very much. Especially my daddy."

"I bet she did. She looks very beautiful." So beautiful in fact, it would be hard for any woman to compete with that.

"Yes. Which is why you should leave," Lucy continued.

"Lucy!" Noah's voice sounded from the top of the stairs. He came down swiftly. "You know better than to be rude to our guests."

Lucy sighed and stood. "Tess needs to go home, Daddy. 'Cause it is really late."

"Past your bedtime, certainly," Noah agreed sternly. He held out his hand to his oldest daughter. "Let's go."

She shuffled to obey. "What about the twins?"

"They are already tucked in. Now what do you say to our guest?"

"Sorry."

She clearly did not mean it.

But to Tess's relief, her dad let it go.

The two moved back up the stairs. Her heart went out to the petulant child. It couldn't have been easy, losing her mother at such a young age. Lucy probably still missed Shelby terribly, just as Tess still missed her own mother, close to a decade after her mom's death. The last thing Tess wanted was to somehow make things worse for Lucy. If her presence here was going to be a problem for the grieving child, she knew she would have to find other accommodation. But in the meantime, there were still chores to be done. Tess finished folding her laundry, and then went into the kitchen to check on the cast iron skillet she'd put in the oven. To her delight, the re-seasoning process was finished and it was ready. She pulled out the baking sheet that the heavy skillet was sitting on and set it on the stove.

Once again, Noah was back, looking embarrassed. "Sorry about what happened earlier," he said gruffly.

This time, Tess's heart went out to them both. Not sure whether or not he wanted to talk about it further, she lifted a hand and said, "Totally understandable—no apology necessary."

Not surprisingly, he still seemed to think there was. Noah let out what might have been a sigh, then scrubbed a hand over his face, before once again meeting Tess's eyes. "I'd like to say it's just because she is overtired tonight," he said candidly, "but the truth is," Noah paused and frowned again, "Lucy can be pretty mercurial."

Was that a warning of more temper tantrums to come? Tess wasn't sure. She did need to ask. "Is my being here going to make things more difficult for her—or you? Because if it is…" Tess paused sincerely. "I'm sure I can find somewhere else to bunk while still checking in on Miss Coco, twice daily, like we agreed."

Noah vetoed that idea with a shake of his head. "That won't be necessary," he told her gruffly. "Lucy knows very well that no matter how grumpy or out of sorts she might be feeling, she still has to treat others kindly and use her manners, and I promise you, even if I have to gently remind her at times, that she will."

His weary expression had her feeling empathy for him, all over again. Struggling against the need to comfort him with a touch, she gave him her most understanding smile. "And I promise you, I won't take offense. I know she is just a kid, and she's doing the best she can, the way we all are."

He nodded and drew another breath. "Thanks."

Tingling from the near contact, Tess turned back to the stove. Suddenly wondering, she asked, "Is it okay if I leave this skillet here on the stove until it cools? It's going to take a while."

"Sure."

Noah followed her gaze to the gleaming black cast-iron skillet. Then his eyes widened in surprise. "That can't be the one you rescued from Waylon's home."

It had been such a sentimental find for her, refurbishing it had been at the top of her list of chores. Tess smiled, relieved to have something a little easier to talk about. "It is, actually."

The awkwardness between them faded as he surveyed the pan from all angles, clearly impressed. "I can't believe it. It looks brand-new."

"Doesn't it?" Tess said proudly.

He moved closer, inspecting it with interest. His tall body radiated both heat and strength. He sent her an approving sidelong glance before moving away once again. "How did you get all the rust off?"

She watched him go with just a tinge of disappointment. "I used table salt and steel wool, and a lot of elbow grease. Then I seasoned it with oil and put it in the oven to cure."

Looking finally ready to hang out and take a breath, he sprawled in a kitchen chair, long legs stretched out in front of him. "Amazing."

Trying not to think how sexy he looked, even doing practically nothing, she tilted her head at him. Refusing to notice how attracted she was to him, she asked, "You've never cooked in cast iron?"

"No." He lifted his arms over his head, stretched languidly. "My mom and sisters do, but I never knew how they cleaned them up." Lazily, he dropped his arms to his sides. Smiled. "You obviously do."

Tess roamed the large state-of-the-art space restlessly, not sure what she should do now that he and the girls were home again. Hide in her room? Or stay downstairs and finish her laundry? Because she still had a load in the dryer...

Figuring the best thing to do was just play it casual, too, she continued, "My mom was an executive chef for some of the best restaurants in Denver.

Mostly French cuisine. All very chichi. But when she was home, which wasn't all that often, she often talked about the food she'd eaten, growing up, that her mother had prepared in her cast-iron skillet."

Noah tilted his head in the direction of the stove top. "You think that's the one?"

"I do. I just think it hadn't been cared for properly or used in a very long time. Which is a shame." Hence, she had needed to bring it back to life, ASAP, as a way of honoring both her grandmother and her mother.

He pushed out of his chair, sauntered over to the fridge and pulled out a beer. Wordlessly, he offered her one. She shook her head. He shut the door behind him and twisted off the cap. Lounging against the counter, he asked, "So you know how to cook in it, then?"

"Oh, yeah. My mom had a whole set of cast iron, and a nice set of stainless-steel cookware, too. Plus, chef's knives, and so on. I inherited it all when she died of pneumonia, my first year of vet school." A lump rose in Tess's throat. Tears stung the back of her eyes. Funny, how things could still hurt. Even nearly a decade later.

He put his drink aside and moved to give her a comforting hug. "Sorry." He squeezed her shoulders companionably, then admitted thickly, "I know firsthand how hard it is to suffer a loss like that. I lost both my parents, too."

It took a moment for what he had said to sink in. Tess did a double take.

He picked up his drink and took another sip. "My sibs and I are all adopted. Our biological parents perished in a fire, after lightning struck our home in the middle of the night, when I was about Lucy's age."

And she thought *she'd* had it bad. She gave in to impulse and hugged him, too, just for a moment. "That sounds really traumatic," she murmured, stepping back.

He nodded in confirmation, then continued reluctantly, "My parents got us all out, to safety, but then went back in for a few things after the rain put the fire out...or so they thought. A spark ignited the gas water heater, which was in the attic. The whole place exploded. They were killed instantly."

"Oh, my God, Noah, I am so sorry."

He moved out of touching range, took another long sip of beer. "It was a long time ago."

"Still, it must have been really tough."

Sorrow came and went in his eyes. Replaced by cool acceptance. "You're right. It was." His expression became even more bleak. "All of us kids were split up into different foster homes, and it was a few years before Carol and Robert were able to get permission from the court to adopt us all."

He shook off his low mood and straightened. "Anyway, that's one reason I don't ever like to put off until tomorrow anything that could be done today. Like," he said, his expression turning warm and welcoming once again, "ensuring you're comfortable. So what else do you need to really settle in? Dinner?

Because my mom sent a huge plate of leftovers in case you hadn't eaten."

It was going to be really hard to keep her guard up, if he was so generous and helpful all the time. She reminded herself this was a short-term arrangement. Meant to be kept businesslike. So why was it feeling like it could be something *more*?

She flashed a smile. "Thanks. That was nice of her. But I'm good. I stopped for a sandwich on my way out of town."

Without warning, his brow furrowed. "Did you have a chance to check on Miss Coco?"

His concern for the animal was laudable. "Yes. She's doing fine."

His eyes turned a mesmerizing blue. "Looking any closer to…?"

Tess cut off his question with a definitive shake of her head. "I still think what I did last night, that it will be another week or two. Possibly even a little more. We will just have to wait and see."

Noah, who was so calm and competent in all other situations, abruptly looked tense and ill-at-ease. Knowing he was as out of his element birthing pets, as she was caring for kids, she touched his arm, her fingers curling around his bicep. "It really is going to be okay," she soothed.

He leaned into her grip. "Promise me?" he rasped.

Trying not to imagine what it would be like to have those strong arms wrapped around her, Tess said, "I promise."

Chapter Five

The vow hung in the air between them. Fragile. Unexpected. Connecting...

The closeness they'd felt all day turned into a wave of white-hot heat. Tess felt herself moving inevitably toward him at the same time he moved toward her. The next thing she knew, his head was lowering. His lips captured hers. A powerful current swept through her, filling her with warmth and need.

It had been so long since she had been held like this. So long since she had felt so wanted and needed. So desired. She opened her lips to the insistent pressure of his. The masculine taste of him overwhelmed her. With a soft moan, she wreathed her arms around his neck. In turn, he wrapped his arms around her and pulled her so close they were one. Her breasts molded to the hardness of his chest, and she succumbed to the erotic sweep of his tongue. Wanting more, until their hearts beat in tandem. Lower still, there was a building pressure and a tingling that stole her breath. And still the tender yet erotic kiss continued, magically showing her what could be, if only she could find the courage to open up her heart...

Noah hadn't meant to put the moves on Tess. They had an agreement, after all. Neither one of them was looking for a relationship. Their lives were full enough already. Yet, the time he'd spent with her over the last two days, the ease with which she'd slipped into his life, the soft surrender of her body and tenderness of her lips as they melted against him left him wondering. Was his lack of regret over this embrace a sign that he was beginning to feel ready to move on from Shelby? To be physically and emotionally close to a woman again? All he knew for certain was that Tess felt so good, so right, in his arms. Their kiss so hot and enticing.

And that was, of course, when she moaned again, this time in trepidation, and placed her palms against his chest.

Abruptly glad one of them had some common sense, he lifted his head. Moved back on a short exhalation of breath, and she did the same.

He read the regret on her pretty face. A tinge of disappointment swept through him.

Her hand flew to her mouth. Pink color filled her cheeks. "I'm sorry," she said.

Strangely enough, Noah wasn't. He might not be

quite ready to go all-in with this woman, but their encounter had felt all kinds of fantastic.

Tess shook her head as if that would clear it. She pressed her fingertips to her damp, kiss-swollen lips. A mixture of remorse and wonder shone in her sage-green eyes. "I don't know what came over me!" She turned away as if they hadn't just shared an embrace that had rocked his world. "I guess it's just all the emotion of the past week or so," she said, as if explaining to a gullible newbie. "It caught up with me. And—and…"

She was so distressed, he had to help her out. Even if what he was going to say to soothe her embarrassment wasn't quite true. It was all he could do not to take her all the way back in his arms and kiss her again, just to prove their heated reaction to each other hadn't been an anomaly. "Left you unexpectedly wanting some comfort?" he guessed kindly. Knowing even if she didn't, this was not as calamitous as she was making it out to be.

Tess blinked. "Yes…that must be it! In any case, it will never happen again." She ran both hands through her hair. Her chest rose and fell with each agitated breath she drew. She huffed in embarrassment. "So how about we just pretend this never happened?"

Not sure how that was going to work, Noah watched her whirl away from him and march back to the mudroom, retrieve her folded laundry and dart up the stairs. Moments later, the guest-room door shut quietly. And that was the last he saw of her that evening.

* * *

"How's that?" Noah's brother Travis asked, the following afternoon.

Noah studied the black-and-white image on his phone. "Maybe a little farther back."

Travis nodded in understanding.

A handyman and cowboy, he was the go-to sibling for any domestic conundrum. Although neither of them had ever done anything like this before, Noah thought.

Travis moved the ladder, climbed back up and held the nanny cam against the stall wall.

Suddenly, Noah could see everything he needed to see. "Perfect," he said.

In quick order, Travis whipped the drill out of his tool belt and finished putting it up. While he removed the ladder, Noah went across the aisle to get Miss Coco, who had been temporarily housed in another stall.

The miniature donkey looked unhappy. The way she always did when there were loud, unfamiliar noises.

He paused to pet her, then led her back to her normal stall.

"She looks uncomfortable," Travis noted.

Her pregnant belly was awfully big, Noah thought, sympathizing. "Yeah, I think she wants to get this over with as much as we do."

His brother teased, "*We* meaning you and the girls…or you and Tess?"

He'd had enough of this at his parents' the evening before. Everyone in his family wanted to see him paired up again. Irritation grew. "Don't start."

"Hey." Travis collapsed the ladder. "You can't deny there are sparks between you and the lovely new vet. We all saw them when we were clearing out her house yesterday. Plus, you arranged to put her up here for the next few weeks or so."

Yes, he had. And it seemed like a fine idea. Until he had ended up kissing her, she had kissed him back and then run away. Only to exit the ranch early this morning again, this time before any of them had gotten up.

She had left him a note, though. Documenting their donkey's continued good health. "That's for Miss Coco's sake."

Travis chuckled with the ease of a happily married man. "Keep telling yourself that."

They walked out of the barn together. Travis put the construction ladder back on his truck while Noah shut the door behind them. The winter day was sunny and surprisingly warm, for January. In the distance, they could see his three girls playing with his sister Jillian's three triplet daughters, with Jillian supervising.

Noah figured it might not be a bad idea to get some feedback. Up 'til now, he'd had zero interest in even spending time with a woman, one-on-one, never mind getting close to her. Feeling incredibly blessed to have the help of two of his siblings today, Noah turned back to Travis. "And, anyway," he huffed, "she's not interested." Which was probably good, since it had been several years since he had been on a date and was more than a little rusty.

Travis raised an eyebrow. "Didn't look that way to any of us," he countered mildly.

Noah ran a hand over his forehead, wishing he hadn't given in to the unexpected wave of desire and chased her away. He grimaced, reviewing the depth of his mistake. "Yeah, well, I tested the waters yesterday." Once again, moving way too recklessly, way too soon. Just as he had since he was a kid and his whole world had gone to ashes in a single moment.

"Tested the waters," Travis echoed, his brow furrowed. "In what way?"

Ruefully, Noah recalled, "We kissed."

Travis mulled over that statement. "You kissed her? Or she kissed you?"

"Both." And it had been fantastic, for as long as it lasted, anyway. Which, in retrospect, seemed not nearly long enough.

Travis shrugged. "Sounds promising to me."

It had been. Until reality sunk in. And it was reality he had to deal with now, like it or not. Noah grimaced, then admitted, "She apologized. And said we should just forget it ever happened."

Travis clapped a reassuring hand on Noah's shoulder. "But you can't," his brother noted happily.

Worse. He didn't *want* to forget it.

Tess had made him feel alive. Their kiss had brought him joy. Made him want to burst out of his self-imposed shell.

They continued on across the lawn, toward Jillian and the six little girls, who were all rowdy as could be. Why couldn't his life be that simple, Noah wondered, as he watched them race around the lawn.

"Want my opinion?" Travis asked.

Noah squinted, considering. Travis had hit the lottery with his wife, Skye, and their son, Robbie. "Maybe."

"You've always been one to follow your instincts, which are pretty damn good, by the way. You've also never been one to sit around and wait for things to happen to you. So if something in you wants to explore the sparks between you and Tess Gardner, then I say go for it."

"It's not that simple, bro. I've got the girls to consider." Their feelings had to count in this, too.

Travis nodded solemnly. "I get that, believe me. And I know Lucy, Avery and Angelica will always be your first priority. But why not give the pursuit everything you've got and see where things lead?" He exhaled slowly, giving Noah a look full of sad remembrance. "Because our family knows better than most how life can change in an instant. And there's nothing worse than looking back, thinking, if only I'd done what I should or could have done... and didn't."

On Sunday afternoon, Tess spent an hour walking the property with the husband-and-wife contractor team recommended to her. "So how long do you think it will take?" she asked when they had returned to the first floor, which, despite the warmer weather outside, was still as cold as a tomb.

Molly looked at Chance. Then the extensive notes she had made. She did most of the design work and scouting of materials. Her husband handled the general contracting. "Three weeks, if everything goes according to plan," she predicted finally.

"Four, if it doesn't," Chance said. "And even then…we should be able to get you in comfortably."

The attractive thirtysomething couple seemed very capable. "That's great!" Tess said, relieved. She smiled at the duo, ready to get going. "Where do I sign?"

Casually, Molly slid her clipboard back into her bag. "I'll email you the contract with the written bid later this evening. You can docu-sign it, and we'll get our crew started."

They left and Tess glanced at her watch. It was barely three o'clock. She still had two errands to do, and then she really needed to head back to the Welcome Ranch and face Noah. Yes, they had kissed… impulsively…and it had been a reckless mistake. One she foolishly kept reliving in her way-too-romantic heart.

She still had to face him sometime. Find a way to move their acquaintance permanently to the friendship phase. Because the last thing she wanted was another failed romance with a man who'd told her from the very beginning what he was, and wasn't, interested in. And while she now realized maybe she wasn't as immune to romance as she had thought,

Noah still had no room in his life for anything but his work and his kids.

Yes, there were sparks between them. Powerful sparks. But it would be foolish to pursue that chemistry, since up to now, anyway, she had never been able to make love, without first being in love.

Hence the safe path was the one she and Noah had started out on—the one that would keep them strictly platonic friends.

Resolved, Tess turned her attention to the errands, still waiting to be done. Both took a little longer than expected.

An hour and a half later, Tess turned her Tahoe into the lane leading up to the ranch. Noah's Expedition was parked next to the house. She parked on the other side of him, then got out and walked over to the barn. By the time she had finished checking on Miss Coco and returned to her SUV, Noah was coming out of the back of the house.

He looked good. *Too good* really, in jeans, boots, a casual sweater and open down jacket that made the most of his broad shoulders and muscular chest.

Suddenly, all she could think about was the kiss they had shared last night, and how much she wanted to do it again.

He was watching her curiously, as if trying to read her mind, while she worked to keep her emotions at bay. "Did you have a good day?"

"Yeah." Finding his steady regard a little unnerving, Tess turned away. She got her carryall out of her SUV and walked around the back to the cargo area.

Then she pushed the button to activate the lift gate. "I wanted to spend some time at the clinic, acquainting myself with their computer systems. Rather than do it tomorrow. So I spent the bulk of the day doing that."

"Makes sense."

"And then I met with contractors and had a little shopping to do."

"Wow, you have been busy."

Unfortunately, the near constant activity had not kept him, or the sizzling hot kiss they had shared, entirely off her mind.

The back of her car opened.

Oblivious to the wistful nature of her thoughts, he looked at the paper grocery sacks stashed inside. "Need some help with any of that?"

"Sure." Tess smiled with a casualness she couldn't begin to feel. "If you're offering."

He took the heavier ones. She carried the bread and eggs. "What's all this for?" he asked mildly, matching his strides to hers.

"As long as I'm staying here, I want to pitch in with some of the food costs. Help out financially in any way I can, to earn my keep, so to speak." They had agreed to each do their own thing, while she was under his roof. But it didn't mean she wanted to freeload off his groceries, day after day. Worse, have things in the fridge taking up space that were off-limits to everyone else. Which was why she had also purchased kid- and family-friendly items.

"You don't have to do that," he told her solemnly, his tall frame radiating barely leashed energy. Together, they mounted the steps that led to the mud-room entrance, close to the driveway. "But, sure… whatever you like."

Happy he hadn't taken offense, Tess released a long, slow breath. She always felt better when she was at her most independent. "Thank you." She waited while he transferred the bags to one arm and opened the back door. He held the door for her, in-herently gallant as ever.

She caught a whiff of his soap and man scent as she passed. Trying not to think about the way he looked at her—as if she was the most fascinating woman on the planet—she carried her things to the island and set them down.

Tess shrugged out of her coat, and at the same time he ditched his. Figuring this was the best time to ask, she looked over at him, surprised at how happy she already felt, even though she was in a new town, with a currently unlivable house, about to start a new job. She traded relaxed glances with him. "In the meantime, I wondered if it would be okay, later tonight, when the girls are in bed and you're done in the kitchen for the night, if I baked a few things to take to work in the morning. Just as an I'm-glad-to-be-here gift for the staff?"

He watched her unload her groceries. "I'm sure your new coworkers would appreciate it." He took the empty bags, efficiently folding them for later re-purposing. "And, of course, it's okay for you to use the kitchen."

"Thanks." Still wondering if she was going to

eventually end up feeling as much of a nuisance here as she had in other places, in her past, she asked, "Where are the girls, by the way?" It was awfully quiet around here.

He turned, nodding at the living area adjacent to the kitchen. She followed his glance and saw the girls sprawled out over the sectional sofa in the living room. The twins were cuddled up together. Lucy was snuggled next to Tank. All were sound asleep.

"Oh, gosh," she whispered in chagrin. "You should have told me. I wouldn't have been speaking so loudly."

Noah shook his head and continued in a normal tone. "I want them to start waking up. If they sleep much longer, there will be no getting them to bed tonight. And they've all got to get up early tomorrow. The twins go to preschool. Lucy attends the elementary school in town."

Just like the two of them both had work. And would need to get their rest, too. "Ah. Right."

Abruptly, she noticed everything else she had missed, given how focused she had been on the tall, ruggedly handsome man at her side. Noah's computer was on, all four of his big displays lit up. The fragrance of fresh-brewed coffee hung in the air. A mug was on his desk. He'd clearly been working on something, while his daughters slept.

Once again, Tess felt like she was intruding.

She hated feeling that way.

And there was only one way to feel like less of an added burden to his already full life. "Actually, I was going to go down to the stable and check on Miss Coco and then go upstairs to catch up on some veterinary journal articles I've been meaning to read."

He looked relieved. Tess slipped out the back door, vet bag in hand.

Three hectic hours later, after the kids were in bed, and Tess was finally able to come downstairs without feeling that she was likely to be in the way, she reflected on what a marathon it had been.

"Are your evenings always like that?" she asked Noah curiously, getting out the things she needed to make her baked goods.

Though she hadn't been there to see the high-spirited activity, she had certainly overheard it. From the time they woke up, cranky and out of sorts from a too-late-in-the-day nap, to the wild, out-of-control giggles and jumping on the beds, when it was time for them to be tucked in, the three girls had been going nonstop.

She couldn't imagine how Noah did it all alone, on top of running the company he'd founded. While still maintaining the patience of a saint.

He paused to gather up three insulated lunch bags from the pantry. "Sometimes it's calm."

She'd never seen a man quite so gentle. And loving. She imagined he had been the same way with his late wife. "But not tonight."

He shrugged his broad shoulders affably, then went to the fridge and got out cheese, fruit and bread. "They've had an unusually hectic four days. Starting Thursday after school, when my parents came over to stay with them so I could go to Fort Worth to meet with a trucking company that wants us to design a cloud-based asset-management platform that will track all their inventory plus shipments, vehicles, drivers, deliveries and so forth in real time. When finished, it will be installed as an app on everyone's phones."

"Sounds...complicated." Impressively so.

He nodded in satisfaction. "It is definitely a new direction for us. One that I think will give Lockhart Solutions much more potential for growth. Although we still plan to keep designing apps that improve everyday life."

"Is that what that is—" Tess gestured at the four monitors in his work area, with what appeared to be computer coding flashing on the screens "—all about?"

He stopped making sandwiches. "No. That's another project I have going. I'll show you." Tess followed as he went over to the desktop, typed in a command and pulled up a security-camera shot of Miss Coco's stall, then got out his cell phone. Another few clicks and the same photo appeared on that.

"Travis was here this afternoon and he helped me install cameras and motion detectors with ambient lighting. So whenever Miss Coco is up and around, I'll get a message and know. And can check on her."

"It looks like Miss Coco is sleeping peacefully now." The miniature donkey had also been fine when

Tess had gone out to the stable to check on her. She wondered if there was something that had happened to precipitate this. Something Noah hadn't told her about yet. "Was there a problem earlier?"

He tilted his head to one side and gave her an easy grin. "Just in how we set it up."

As he came closer, she noticed he smelled like kids' bubble bath and shampoo. Patches of his shirt were damp, too, from where the kids had splashed him.

She had never imagined a single dad could be so sexy. Yet, here he was. Looking completely worse for wear. And all she wanted to do was haul him close and kiss him again. Even more passionately this time. She swallowed around the parched feeling in her throat. "I don't understand."

"The alert on my phone goes off every time Miss Coco moves or rolls over or gets up to get a drink, which is a lot more often than I knew. Anyway, I need to put a timer on the app I wrote for this, so it will only alert me if she's up for five minutes or more at a time—"

Tess interrupted, "Make it ten."

The intensity in his dark blue eyes deepened.

Knowing that if she stood there next to him like that for much longer, they'd end up kissing again, she went back to the kitchen.

Squinting, he stayed where he was, phone still cradled in his big hand. "Are you sure?"

Aware she was tingling again, with yearning this time, Tess went back to grating icy cold butter into small chunks.

Scones.

She was making scones…

And they needed to turn out right.

Which meant she had to focus on what she was doing, not him.

"I'm positive." Glad for the physical distance between them, she looked over at him again, to make her point. "Unless you want to drive yourself absolutely crazy."

Judging by the depth of his scowl, he did not.

"Okay, well that's easily doable." Oblivious to the way she was still admiring everything about him, he sat down in front of the computer and made several changes on screen. Then stood with a satisfied exhalation of breath. "Done."

He strode back into the kitchen to join her and went back to assembling school lunches for the girls.

She was working at the opposite end of the island, to make sure they each had plenty of personal space. "So what are you making?" he asked.

Happy to have something to concentrate on besides the attractive single dad opposite her, Tess began folding the grated butter into the flour mixture. "Scones. Vanilla, blueberry, apricot and peach."

With heavy lidded eyes, he watched her add vanilla and cream, then knead it in with her hands. His gaze drifted over her contemplatively before returning with slow deliberation to her eyes. "Smells good." He gave her a panty-melting smile. "And they aren't even in the oven yet."

Reminded of what a sensual activity cooking together could be, Tess let out a pent-up breath. She could tell he was remembering their kiss. Maybe even longing for another one. There was no way they were going to end up in each other's arms again. *No way.*

Determined to keep her boundaries firmly in place, she avoided looking at him directly and reassured him cheerfully, "Not to worry." She patted the crumbly dough into a round circle, then cut it into eighths. "I planned to leave a sampling of the four different types for you and the girls."

She reached for the parchment-lined baking sheets, irritated he was making her feel all kinds of things she most certainly did not want to experience right now. Like the absence of love and family and joy in her life. She was a vet, for heaven's sake! Shouldn't she at least have a pet?

With a huff, she added, "If they like scones, that is."

The compassion in his regard sent another thrill racing through her. "I am sure they will," he told her.

Beginning to realize she was going to have to keep herself very physically busy to avoid more moments like this, moments that could tempt them into intimacy, Tess slid the first pan of scones into the oven.

Resolved, she swung back to face him. "You know, I don't have to limit my contribution to caring for animals and buying groceries while I'm bunking here. I could pitch in with household chores, fold laundry, even cook a little, too, if it would help out." Ease his burden a little bit. And give him more time to simply enjoy spending time with his three adorable little girls. Instead of juggling everything all at once.

Chapter Six

Noah regarded Tess silently, not sure how to respond to her offer to help out even further. The interested side of him was all in. But the widowed single dad? He knew it was never going to be that easy. Especially with Lucy still running hot and cold. She was okay with Tess being there one moment, then indifferent and or resentful the next.

Trying hard not to think about what he would really like to do, which was forget about everything but the two of them, wrap her in his arms and kiss her until dawn, he tamped down his desire with effort and met her eyes. Then he asked casually, "What happened to the idea we would each do our own thing?"

Which would have eliminated this problem entirely. And made life a whole lot more boring.

Oblivious to his thoughts, and already back on

task, Tess was chopping up fruit for the next batch of scones. She had twisted her hair into a loose sexy knot on the back of her head when she'd begun to cook. The butterscotch curls spilled out over the butterfly clip. Loose strands brushed her cheeks and the nape of her neck. She did not seem to have any idea how sexy she looked, but he did. Boy, did he ever.

Ignoring the pressure building at the front of his jeans, he went back to making school lunches. With a shrug, she continued, "It probably would've worked great if it were just the two of us." Her delicate hands moved with laudable expertise as she completed each culinary task, making him wonder how those same skilled fingers would feel on him.

She leaned toward him slightly. "But it's not, Noah." She drew a conflicted breath and went on matter-of-factly, making her case. "And with all that needs to get done around here, it seems selfish and self-centered of me to hide out in the guest suite when I am on the ranch. Instead of coming down here and pitching in and helping out."

Damn, she was generous. And kind. And smart. And pretty. Plus, all the things he yearned for in a woman, and expected to never have again, after Shelby passed. Yet, here he was, feeling like maybe it was time for him to open up his heart again. Even as the cautious side of him said things were fine as they were. And resolutely warned against bringing a new woman into their midst.

Noticing she was still waiting for his response, he cleared his throat, said carefully, "I see your point."

The color in her cheeks deepened—as if she sensed his rejection coming. She went back to shredding cold butter on the box grater. "Then…?"

He pushed aside his desire to get even closer to her, close enough to make love and share confidences, and said kindly instead, "I wish it was that simple, Tess—but it's not. Nothing is when it comes to my girls." And me. "So," he told her regretfully, "I'd like to stick to our original agreement and keep things as casual and separate as possible."

Tess's hands stilled. He couldn't tell if she was disappointed or relieved. Her feelings were definitely hurt. As he had half suspected they would be when he turned down her offer. Wanting her to understand where he was coming from, he continued, "We had a nanny in California. We hired her when Shelby first got sick and kept her on even after she finished her cancer treatment, because frankly we really needed the help." He exhaled, his lips compressing as he recollected sorrowfully, "Carrie stayed with us that first year after Shelby died, and it really helped because she was able to bring a woman's touch into the household and fill the void that my wife's death left." Noah sighed. "But she didn't want to move to Texas with us because her fiancé and all her family were in California." He shook his head, recalling grimly. "The girls were really distraught. In a sense it was like losing Shelby all over again and they cried for weeks. And I don't want them to get too attached to anyone outside the family again."

Tess's slender body relaxed. She nodded sympathetically, understanding.

He watched her fold wet ingredients into dry with the same easy skill she seemed to do everything else. He could only imagine how that dexterity would transmit to lovemaking.

Forcing himself to get back on track, he closed up the reusable lunch sacks and admitted wearily, "I also don't want Lucy jumping to any conclusions."

Her delicate brow pleated. Her gaze drifted over him. "Because Lucy is opposed to you dating anyone?"

Worse. With brutal honesty, he explained how deep the hurt in him and his girls went. Not a one of them wanted to love and lose again. "Because Lucy wants her mom back and that can't happen. And anything that points that out to her again is painful to her," Noah concluded gruffly.

Which made it painful for the rest of them, too.

Tess was in her office at the vet clinic late Monday afternoon, making notes on the patients she had seen that day, when Sara stopped in. The rest of the staff had already left, so the building was quiet, with the dark of midwinter descending outside.

"Everything go okay for you today?" the managing partner asked.

Tess nodded happily. "It was a great first day on the job, thanks."

Sara eased into a chair, resting a hand on her pregnant belly. "How's the rest of your situation going?"

Tess explained the deal she had made with Noah over the weekend. To keep watch over the donkey, until the birth, whenever that happened. And then stay on for as long as needed until momma and baby were doing well, the imprint training completed and he was sure he could handle them on his own.

Sara did some quick calculations. "So you'll likely be living at Welcome Ranch until mid-February?"

Tess nodded. "Thereabouts. At least that's the plan. I just hope the renovation gets done in four weeks, as promised…" She talked about her meeting with the married contractors she had hired, who were reputedly the very best in the area. Especially when it came to kitchen and bathroom design.

"Not to worry. Molly and Chance don't make promises they can't keep. They will finish on schedule. Meanwhile, we both need to lock up and get out of here."

Knowing her coworker was right, Tess stood.

Sara walked her out. "The scones were delicious, by the way. Everyone loved them."

Recalling the culinary lessons she had received in her youth, Tess admitted, "My mom used to say food made with love is the ultimate icebreaker."

Sara's smile bloomed. "Your mom was right. Speaking of which, my husband, Matt, is making his famous chili and cornbread tomorrow evening. You want to come for dinner with us and the kids? See our ranch?"

"Love to." She needed more friends in Laramie County, so she wouldn't be constantly feeling the need to lean on Noah, for all things, big and small.

Tess got in her Tahoe and drove out to the Welcome Ranch. Noah was pacing the porch, on what appeared to be some sort of business call. He gave her a curt nod, and turned his back, continuing to grimly troubleshoot some problem. Inside, dinner prep appeared to be temporarily halted. The girls were close to a meltdown.

"We're hungry!" Angelica said.

Her twin Avery nodded. "Super hungry."

Lucy scowled. "Whenever Daddy gets that look on his face, it's going to be forever before he gets off the phone."

Tess took off her coat and ventured another glance outside. Noah did indeed look completely wrapped up in whatever was going on.

Not willing to just stand around and do nothing when the kids needed to be fed, she headed into the kitchen. She turned the flame on under the big pot of water. "So what were you going to have?"

"Spaghetti with butter and parm for the twins and spaghetti with red sauce and meatballs for me and Daddy," Lucy said.

The latter appeared to have been simmering on the back burner, but had been turned off. She adjusted the flame back to simmer.

All three girls climbed up on the stools at the island, to watch. "Do you know how to cook?" Avery asked.

Tess nodded, acutely aware this was not part of the deal she had made with Noah just the night before. "I do. My mom was an executive chef, and she taught me how when I was a kid. It was the only way we could spend a lot of time together."

"'Cause she worked a lot, just like our daddy?" Angelica murmured.

"That's right. But that's what parents have to do, you know—work so they can take care of their families." Especially single parents, like her mom and Noah. Like it or not, they had a lot to juggle.

And sometimes, despite their best efforts, they needed help.

Even if it wasn't from a big, extended, loving family, but the relative stranger/houseguest who just happened to be there.

Lucy studied her with open curiosity. "I used to cook with my mommy."

"We didn't," Avery announced with a beleaguered sigh. "We were too little."

"Just babies," Angelica said.

Tess smiled at the trio of girls, who were no longer fussing with each other and complaining. She could really get used to coming home nightly to this eager little fan club. "Do you-all cook with your dad?"

They shook their heads in disappointment. "Not really," Lucy said. "He's too impatient and he says he's not good at explaining things in the kitchen."

Tess understood.

Teaching one child to cook was one thing.

Monitoring all three of his lively little girls with their differing skill sets, probably another.

"I can help you tonight, though," Lucy said. "Just like I used to help my mommy."

"We're big enough, too, now," Avery claimed.

"Yes, we are," Angelica agreed.

Tess looked over at their eager expressions.

Oh boy, she was really getting into it, pushing past boundaries now, but Noah was still outside pacing and talking on the phone. And honestly, dinner did have to get made, the kids kept entertained so they wouldn't be interrupting him.

"You know what?" She looked at the ingredients on the counter. "I think that we could all make a salad together. You up for that?" she asked.

"Yes!" all three girls said in unison.

Tess rinsed the greens and then showed them how to tear up the romaine leaves into little pieces and put them in individual wooden salad bowls.

They were just adding croutons and shavings of parmesan cheese when Noah came back in.

He was off the phone. And when he saw what they were doing, he did not look happy. Not at all.

Noah knew, even as his temper flared, that he was overreacting to the sight of Tess making dinner with his kids. It wasn't as if she was vying for the position of their mom, or his next wife.

Far from it.

Yet the sight of her, still in her vet-clinic scrubs, looking so pretty as she charmed and entertained his daughters, hit him square in the solar plexus.

He'd thought he was doing fine on his own.

But it wasn't true, he admitted ruefully. Because if it was, Avery, Angelica and Lucy would look this happy all the time. They didn't. Which meant he still had work to do. And an example to set.

Fortunately, the deeply ingrained manners instilled in him as a kid made it easy to invite her to join them and make small talk throughout the meal. Most of which was focused on the kids and their days at school.

Not surprisingly, Tess avoided direct eye contact with him and made herself scarce after dinner, staying only long enough to help him clear the dishes before heading down to the stable to check on Miss Coco.

Figuring they would talk this out later, he took the girls upstairs, shepherded them through the bath and bedtime routines and read them their stories. When he finally finished around eight o'clock, and went to find her, the door to the guest suite stood open. The room was dark and empty.

Downstairs, there was no sign of Tess, either. He went to the security monitor and checked the stable. She wasn't there, either.

Tank was curled up by the back door, as if guarding it. Noah noticed that the back porch lights were on. Tess was sitting outside in her coat, with a small wool blanket drawn across her lap, and was studying a stack of bookmarked magazines.

Knowing he was entitled to be ticked off, yet feeling a little remorseful for his grumpy mood, he walked out onto the back deck. Stepping closer, he exhaled his exasperation.

She slid him a surprised glance.

"What are you doing?" The words were out before he could halt them.

Lips set stubbornly, she went back to the glossy pictures in front of her. "I'm looking over some design possibilities Molly wanted me to peruse. And enjoying my evening."

Enjoying? Really? He surveyed her wind-chapped cheeks and tousled hair. "It's too cold to be sitting outside."

She took a tube of ChapStick out of her pocket and rubbed it across her lips. "Maybe for a native Texan," she quipped.

He returned her challenging look. "Ha! Funny!"

She decided to make a second pass over her soft, luscious lips. "It's thirty-two degrees, cowboy. Which is *nothing* in a Denver winter."

So she was a little ticked off at him, too. For initially behaving like a jerk.

Luckily, he had reined his temper and resentment in.

And hadn't.

He cleared his throat, thinking this discussion would go better inside. "Still…" He stopped, then tried again. "Tess…"

She slid the tube back in her pocket and stood, squaring off with him resolutely. "Look, I know I overstepped my bounds. Continuing to prepare the dinner you started, interacting with your three girls and just generally being in the way of your normal routine."

So she intuitively understood how jarring it had

been for him to walk in and see her doing all the things that Shelby would have been doing.

She stomped a little closer, tilting her head up. "But I have to tell you that I will *always* err on the side of doing what is best for children, and they were hungry and tired and needed to eat. Which they did as soon as I could get it all ready."

He saw how deeply he had insulted her. He lifted both palms in surrender. The last thing he wanted was to fight with her. He'd had way too much of that in his marriage. "I never said…"

She sent him a withering glare. "You don't have to! My dad died in a motorcycle accident before I was even born. So I was the only child of a single mom."

Tess lifted a hand, refusing to let him offer condolences.

Stonily, she continued, "I grew up being foisted on one family friend after another, on the nights when my mom worked as a chef and couldn't get a sitter." Her eyes shone with turbulent emotion. "She usually didn't get by to pick me up until well after midnight. Which meant," Tess continued grimly, "I either had to stay on someone's sofa, or go to sleep on a cot in the restaurant office. Only to be woken up to go home with her."

He thought he'd had a rough childhood. But this… His heart went out to her. "Sounds…awful."

She shrugged away his empathy. "Some of it was. Some of it wasn't."

He watched her drop the magazine she'd been

reading on the stack on the deck table. "What was nice?"

Tess paused, her expression turning sentimental as she recalled with soft reluctance, "Sometimes on the weekends, my mom made us a special midnight dinner at the restaurant, after closing."

That sounded better.

She ran her hands through her hair, pushing the unruly blond strands off her face. "We would talk about our weeks." She released a shuddering breath. "That was always really special."

He watched her pace to the railing and back. "And what wasn't so great?"

She gave him an aggravated look, but to his surprise, answered him, anyway, her low voice roughened with pain. "Me, thinking about spending my entire life wondering if I would ever be important enough to anyone." The edge of her teeth raked her trembling lower lip. "Me—" tears glistened in her eyes "—trying to be patient. To not feel like I was perpetually, always and forever, in someone's way."

Then the tears flowed, flooding her beautiful face. As if it was all suddenly too much for her. Noah knew it was too much for him. He took her in his arms, bringing her against him, and held her close. Suddenly, they were kissing. *Passionately.* Her arms went around his neck. And this lip-lock was even more incredible than their first had been.

With a low moan of appreciation, she pushed against him, going up on tiptoe, better fitting the heat of her slender body against his. Heart racing, he drank in the scent of her, appreciating the sweet, tempting taste of her mouth and lips. She curled against him with a quiet moan, and the kiss turned tender, then feisty, as their bodies heated, and pulsed, and tender again.

Threading his hands through her hair, he kissed her long and hard and deep. She kissed him back, just as fervently, her hands skimming over his shoulders, down his back.

With a soft murmur of acquiescence, she arched against him. Wanting—demanding—more.

His own body hardened.

He could feel her vulnerability, the need that was as intense as his.

What were they doing?

Suddenly feeling like he was taking unfair advantage, he broke off the kiss and lifted his head. She stepped back, looking as emotionally shaken as he felt.

Once again, her defenses were up.

Which was understandable, since neither of them had meant for this to happen.

Guilt flowing through him, he released a breath. Tried to ease the situation with a little humor. "I know, that wasn't in our deal, either," he said wryly.

"Nor should it be." Tess ran a hand through her hair. "The deal we made last night was a smart one. I think we should go back to it."

If he didn't want to end up hurting her, the way he apparently just had, she was probably right. And yet…somehow it felt wrong to pretend nothing was happening, when it clearly was.

He locked gazes with her. Doing his best to give her what she wanted, said, "So each of us should just stick to doing our own thing?"

"Yes. As much as possible," she said stoically.

"Okay," he said, and nodded, even though right now he was selfishly thinking that wasn't what he wanted after all.

While there was no denying he had emotional baggage of his own, what he wanted was to be even closer to her. To see where things might lead…if they allowed the spark between them to fully ignite.

But clearly, she didn't feel the same way.

As if to prove his point, she grabbed her stack of magazines and held them in front of her like a shield, then brushed by him. "Luckily, tomorrow it won't be a problem." She tossed the parting words over her shoulder. "I'm having dinner with Sara and Matt. I won't be home until late, way after your kids are in bed for the night."

Noah was just finishing up another phone call at noon the following day, when he saw his sister Jillian's Lockhart Antique Roses van pull up next to his house.

He and Tank walked out to greet her.

Smiling, she gave him a hug. "I come bearing gifts, as always."

He followed her around to the tailgate. "Food, I hope." The kids loved all the Lockhart women's cooking better than his. And his sisters and mom were always conspiring to make sure he had three or four dinners delivered for him and the kids every week. Things that only had to be put in the oven, or heated on the stove. "So what do we have?" he asked, smiling.

"Chicken tinga in little phyllo cups." She unhooked the latched carrying top on the baking dish to show him. "Heat this in the oven for ten minutes. Then sprinkle lightly with grated cheese and put the tray back in just until the cheese melts. Which will only take another minute or two." She handed him the chicken dish and pulled out a second covered tray. "There's also a veggie-and-fruit tray with ranch and yogurt for dipping."

"Wow. You really went all out."

"Yeah." She tilted her head to study him. "You sounded a little down this morning."

She had called to let him know she had prepared dinner for both their families that night. Because she and her husband, Cooper, had young triplet daughters, their weeknight meals were usually geared for kid palates. If they wanted to do something more gourmet, they always cooked it on the weekends, after the girls were in bed. "A lot of issues at work." Which was true.

Problem was, there were issues at home, too.

And in his romantic life…

And that was new.

Since he hadn't ever figured he would be in a relationship again, he hadn't expected to have to deal with those kinds of issues again. Like the lingering tension that could follow an emotional exchange. Or the frustration that came with the fact they weren't of the same mind. And might not ever really be.

It had been easier to just be a single dad, than worry about perpetually disappointing the woman in his life again.

Until he had met Tess Gardner, anyway...

Jillian made a face that reminded him she had not only started her own business from scratch, but also taken on the emergency guardianship of Cooper's three toddler nieces as well. Only to later adopt them and marry him. And together, they made one hell of a happy family.

She gave him a consoling pat on the arm. "Work comes with issues. For everyone, every day."

She accompanied him into the house, Tank lagging behind them. She paused to hand him her tray and shut the door. "It wasn't that."

Noah carried the meal into the kitchen and slid it all into the fridge. He figured if anyone would understand, it would be Jillian. He added more water to Tank's bowl. "I think I screwed things up with Tess."

His sister took off her coat and got comfortable. She settled on a stool and leaned forward, both arms on the kitchen island. "Tank and I are all ears."

Noah caught her eyeing his electric kettle. He put it on, then got out two mugs and a box of green-tea bags. Hard to explain how Tess had affected him. From the first moment he had laid eyes on her, he had felt an attraction that just would not go away. Instead, it seemed to get more intense every time he saw her.

Aware Jillian was waiting, he tilted his head and said, "Well, things started out a bit rocky."

Her gaze gentled with sisterly understanding. "In what sense?"

"I was trying to be helpful. She didn't trust it. Or me. But then she kind of needed my assistance getting her house cleared out. Finding a place to stay temporarily."

"That hasn't been going well?" she asked.

He paused as he got out the milk and sugar, not sure how much he wanted to reveal. Yet, knowing he had to confide in someone. *"It was."*

Jillian grinned, then guessed, "You kissed her?"

Noah nodded, recalling the lightning bolt of desire that first kiss had sent through him. "More than once, actually."

His sister paused in the act of opening up her tea bag and sliding it into her still-empty mug. "She kiss you back?"

Noah recalled the soft silkiness of Tess's lips, the sweet taste of her mouth. "Ah…yeah."

Jillian sobered, but couldn't quite make her grin disappear. She added a tea bag to his mug, too. "Then I don't see the problem."

Noah brought over the kettle and filled both mugs with steaming water. *There wouldn't have been one if I hadn't panicked.*

He shoved a hand through his hair. In retrospect, he wished he had reacted in any way but the way he had. Swallowing around the knot of remorse in his throat, he admitted, "I told her we should take a step back and avoid getting too involved, because I didn't want the kids to get the wrong idea about us."

Or maybe us to get the wrong idea about us.

"And think that Tess was going to be a permanent part of our family, the way they once thought Carrie, their nanny back in California, was going to be."

Jillian stirred her tea. Was concerned now. "And why would you do that?" she asked kindly. "Given that Tess isn't a nanny or trying to be?"

Noah straightened. "Because the twins really, really like her," he replied, defending himself. "And although her emotions are all over the place, as usual, Lucy's really warming up to her, too."

His sister lifted her mug and sipped. "And you consider that a problem? Especially considering how protective your eldest is?"

Noah tightened his hands around his mug. "Potentially." Because he wasn't the only one who would get hurt in this situation if he screwed up again. The way he had in his marriage when it became clear that he and Shelby did not want the same kind of lifestyle, and the two of them couldn't seem to get along. Unless, of course, Shelby did get exactly what she wanted, when she wanted it. Then she was incredible. Charming. Cheerful. So sweet and giving and attentive to him and the girls and Tank.

Had it not been for her fierce belief in him, there was no way that he would be where he was, professionally, today.

Seeming to know what he was thinking about, Jillian reached over to touch his forearm. "Want my advice?"

He looked at her, nodding.

"I know you've always been a fast-moving kind of guy, who could drop out of college and start his own company at age nineteen. But try not to get so far ahead of yourself this time. Or go borrowing trouble where none may exist."

It was certainly a tempting notion. Noah clinked mugs with her. "Live in the moment?"

Jillian smiled. "Right now, for you, there is no other way."

Chapter Seven

The kids were long in bed, and Noah was on another work phone call Tuesday evening, when Tess
returned to Welcome Ranch around 10:00 p.m. He
saw her get out of her Tahoe and head for the stable,
vet bag in hand. She was in there for about ten or
fifteen minutes then walked back over to the house.

She slipped in the door, gave him a thumbs-up and
headed straight to the guest suite upstairs, while he
tried to formulate a reply to his colleague that didn't
sound anywhere near as distracted as he felt.

The next morning, she slipped back out to the
stables, just as he was leaving to take the girls to
school. When he returned from town, some thirty
minutes later, he was surprised to see her red Tahoe
still parked next to the house.

Concerned, he went to the stable. Miss Coco lifted

a drowsy head to look at him, then nestled right back down in the hay and went back to sleep.

So all was fine there.

Was it fine with Tess?

Worried, he hurried on over to the house. The kitchen was as he had left it, rife with the got-to-get-out-the-door-on-a-school day mess. Tank was upstairs, parked outside her closed bedroom door. Apparently guarding. As if he, too, knew something was out of the ordinary.

Noah stood there, debating.

Going up to see if she was okay would be intruding.

On the other hand, she was normally at the clinic by the time it opened. And it had opened a good hour and a half before. Which meant she wasn't just going in late. She wasn't going in. On day three of her new employment?

Resolved, he went up the stairs. Knocked.

Seconds later, he heard movement on the other side. She swung open the door. She was dressed in worn jeans and a pink-and-blue plaid flannel shirt, her thick curly hair drawn up in a bouncy ponytail at the back of her head. Her fair skin was flawless, save for the pink flush highlighting her sculpted cheeks.

She huffed out an irritated breath. "Yes?"

Okay, so she wasn't glad to see him. But he was determined to stay the course. "I wanted to see if everything was all right."

She slapped her hands on the sexy curves of her

hips. Angled her chin at him. And stared at him with her usual fiery pride. "Why wouldn't it be?"

"You didn't go to work."

Tess squared her slender shoulders and took a deep breath. "I'm working from noon to nine today."

Suddenly it all made sense. Feeling like a fool, he said, "Evening office hours." Which were held four times a week. He knew that because Tank and Miss Coco got their veterinary care there. Although usually someone came out to his ranch, to see Miss Coco.

"Yes." She angled her thumb at the center of her chest, inadvertently drawing his attention to the open vee of her shirt and the soft curves of her breasts. "And I'm the vet seeing patients this evening. So..." She lifted a censuring eyebrow at him. "If that's all..." She started to shut the door.

It wasn't. Still hoping a truce might be possible, if she would just give him a moment, he caught the door with the palm of his hand. "It's not."

She lifted her delicate brow. Another silence fell. They regarded each other warily.

He tried to make amends. "I'm sorry about what happened the other night."

"The kiss, or the immediate brush-off afterward?" she countered coolly.

He remained in the portal, wedged between the door and the frame. "I know what I said came out all wrong."

She continued watching him steadily, an emotion he could not decipher in her expression. "You think?"

Still holding her eyes, he stepped back out of the doorway. Lifting both palms in an age-old gesture of surrender, he offered a contrite nod. "I'd like to start fresh."

She moved away from him. Back ramrod-straight, she sat down on the padded chaise. Then picked up one of her cowgirl boots and held it in her hand. The firestorm of emotion she had been holding back since they had last spoken suddenly sparked in her eyes. "The thing is, Noah, I am not sure that is such a good idea."

Glad she was at least speaking to him again, he said, "Why not?"

That earned him another long, assessing look. Her eyes taking on an unexpected sheen of vulnerability, she pulled on one boot, then the other. With a sigh, she got to her feet once again. Then claimed with a weariness that seemed to come straight from her soul, "Because you are putting me in the same situation I was in with my ex."

Hoping to learn more about what she had loathed about her past, and wanted in her future, he challenged her mildly. "In what way?"

With a shrug, she admitted in a low, pain-edged voice, "Carlton set all the boundaries. Everything had to be done his way. My feelings weren't important. And unless I wanted to fight nonstop, it was just easier to go along with him."

Noah could understand the not-wanting-to-fight part. He hated disagreements, too. Especially the ones he'd had with Shelby that had gone on and on. Completely unnecessarily.

He watched her pace to the window and back, her hips swaying gently. "I find it hard to believe you were ever a pushover," he countered.

She swung back, gaze narrowed. "Well, believe it." She shook her head regretfully. "Part of it was that he had such a forceful personality. We were in vet school together. He was great at organizing vast quantities of material. Whereas I was better at the nuances. So he did all the big-picture stuff, and I worked on the details. It wasn't long before that process slipped into our dating life, too."

Realizing all over again how incredibly gorgeous she was, Noah stepped closer. "When did it start to become a problem?"

She lounged against the bureau, ankles crossed, arms folded in front of her. Hurt mixed with humiliation. "From the beginning." She bit her lip. "I just didn't want to admit it because there was already so much stress, just trying to excel in the rigorous curriculum. I needed someone strong on my team, and he was definitely that. And then when my mother died unexpectedly, of complications of pneumonia, well suffice it to say I needed him more than ever."

His heart going out to her, Noah took up the place next to her. "Did you live together?"

She shook her head, inundating him with her citrus-and-patchouli fragrance. "Not until the end of our last year of residency. Until then, he insisted we each keep our separate places, even though it would have been a lot easier, financially, to share space, since one of us was always sleeping at the other person's place."

He let his gaze drift over the delicately sculpted lines of her face before returning to her sage-green eyes. "What changed?"

"Carlton knew I wanted more of a commitment. He wasn't ready for marriage just yet, so he offered up living together—just as a trial, mind you—along with a proposal and an engagement ring, and I accepted."

"How did it work?"

Tess lifted her slender shoulders in a dismissive shrug. "Fine, I guess. Even though he was opposed to even talking about a wedding date."

"That didn't bother you?"

Sadness came and went in her expression. She sighed. "It did, but…back then, we had been together for well over six years and I was still laboring under the illusion that we would marry one day. We just needed to wait until the time was right." She released a heavy sigh. "But when we both got really nice job offers in different places, I began to see it didn't matter how patient I was. His needs—his *career*—would always take priority over us as a couple. He thought I should do the same. That for both of us, our careers had to come first. We had worked too hard and too long for them not to take precedence."

"So you broke up?"

More regret filled her expression. "We tried to make the long-distance thing work for about six months. But all that did was drive us further apart emotionally. So we called it quits."

He studied the soul-deep weariness reflected on her face. "Which was when?"

She sighed. "About two years ago."

With effort, he tamped down the need to pull her into his arms and kiss her again. "Anyone since?"

She rubbed idly at the denim stretched across her thigh. "I've been concentrating on my career."

"Protecting your heart."

She lifted her gaze to his. The flush in her cheeks deepened. "If that were all I were doing here, cowboy, maybe it wouldn't be so bad."

She was talking about the two of them again. But not in the positive way he hoped. "What else are you doing?"

"The same thing I did in the beginning with my ex. Going all out to make sure you're okay with literally everything going on between us, instead of tending to my own needs."

He knew he'd been running hot and cold with her. He was sorry about that. Sorry he'd let anything interfere with the friendship they had started to forge from that first night.

He also knew this situation they were in was spurred by both their issues. She needed to know that, too. He gazed into her eyes. Seeking forgiveness, peace. "And why would you be doing that?"

With a huff, she pushed away from the bureau. "That's the hell of it. I don't know."

He caught her before she could run away. "I think

you do. I think you're doing that for the same reason I went dashing up the stairs when I got back from town, to make sure you weren't sick or something. Because like it or not, whether we *want* it or not, Tess, there is something between us."

Tess knew, as much as she loathed to admit it, that Noah was right. There was something special and electric and compelling between them. But that didn't necessarily mean they should give in to it. She whirled away from him, putting enough distance between them so they were no longer invading each other's personal space. "Yeah, and here's the part where you kiss me again," she taunted, daring him to make a pass at her again.

His grin widened, as if warning her he was more than eager to accept her challenge. Before she had a chance to back away, he wrapped his arms around her and brought her close enough to feel the heavy thudding of his heart.

She threw up her arms between them, splaying her palms against his chest, picking up steam with every second. Her heart in turmoil, she lifted her chin. "Don't. You. Dare."

His eyes glinted. "Hey, you are the one who brought it up."

Okay, so she had known it was a mistake to throw down the gauntlet with Noah, just as it had been a mistake to have any conversation at all with him when she was this upset. She should be concentrating only on her new job, the house she had inherited.

Which meant she should already be looking for another place to stay in the interim. Even if it was in the stable. Because this—being so close to Noah—wasn't working. All it was doing was reminding her of her own loneliness and, worse, conjuring up feelings of unbidden longing and lust. Tempting her to throw caution to the wind and fall for him.

But it had been *so long* since anyone had looked at her the way he was looking at her now. As if she was the most beautiful woman on earth. As if the best thing for either of them right now would be a temporary fling.

"Well, I didn't mean it."

He tunneled his hands through her hair. "Didn't you?" he countered softly, tilting her face up to his. "Because I could have sworn you did…"

He was so on target with his observation she felt her knees wobble, just a tad. Determined not to let him know how much he was arousing her, Tess huffed, "We've already tested the waters twice. There's no need to test them again."

Noah delivered a slow, heart-stopping smile. "Kiss me again," he demanded, lowering his lips to hers, "and I'll consider it three strikes and I'm out."

Before she could draw a breath, he delivered the most evocative, tantalizing kiss she had ever experienced in her life. She hadn't been prepared for that and shuddered as he deepened the connection, pressing his body up against hers, mingling his tongue with hers. The pleasurable caress wreaked havoc with her carefully built defenses.

She hadn't realized until this moment just how much she needed to be physically touched, loved.

He broke off the kiss and regarded her closely, his eyes darkened and unwavering on hers. He rubbed his thumb across her lower lip. "Tell me to stop," he growled. "And I will never put the moves on you again."

This was her chance to walk away, to end it now. She couldn't. Even though she knew this was crazy. That it could never last. Not when his life was so complicated. Not when the ghost of Shelby loomed between them.

She also knew she wasn't going to be able to just walk away, not with his passion roaring through her, as sudden and fierce as a winter storm. She wanted him as much as he wanted her. She had to get this out of her system.

"Go," she said instead.

His sexy grin widened. She trembled at the raw tenderness in his gaze. "Go?"

She went up on tiptoe, winding her arms about his neck. "Give it all you've got."

"Well, all right then…" Not wasting a single moment, he lowered his mouth to hers and kissed her again. Sensations swept through her, more potently than before. Suddenly, everything she wanted rose to the surface, and everything she'd held back came pouring forth. And what she wanted most was Noah Lockhart. Right here. Right now.

Rising to the challenge, he slid his palms down her spine, rested them on her hips, pressing her lower half to his. She felt the depth of his desire. And still, they kissed. And kissed. Until their hearts pounded in unison and she couldn't think of any place she would rather be. He was hot and hard and male. She wanted him to fill her up and end the aching loneliness deep inside her. To help her live again, *really* live. And if this one interlude was what it took to make it happen, so be it.

Noah hadn't expected Tess would take him up on his offer. But now that she was kissing him back, ardently, he was all in, too. Kissing her again, hot and hard and wet and deep. Until she moved restlessly against him, wanting still more. Raging need sweeping through him, he slipped off her shirt and her bra, removed her boots and unsnapped her jeans. She quivered as denim and panties slid down her silky-smooth thighs. Her hands rested on his broad shoulders while he helped her step out of them.

"So beautiful," he rasped, his thumbs tracing the curves of her breasts, caressing her pink, pouting nipples.

Still kneeling, he savored the sight of her. Then he parted her thighs, felt her with his fingertips and kissed her and stroked her until she was on the brink. Shuddering. Gone.

Unable to wait any longer, he left her side just long enough to retrieve a condom. When he returned, she was already in the bed, waiting. He stripped down, joined her. She watched, mesmerized, as he rolled it on. Then settled between her thighs. Her legs wrapped around his hips and a shaky breath escaped her. And then they were kissing again. She was wet and open. He was hot and pulsing. He took her slowly, allowing her the time to adjust to the weight and size of him, then going deeper still. Her muscles trembled, tensed. She let her hand slide down his spine to his hips, bringing him inside her more intimately. And then, there was no more waiting, no more wondering. Only feeling, and the inevitable buildup of passion and sensations that ended with her falling apart in his arms, and him following. Together, they hung together suspended in incredible pleasure.

Eventually, their breathing slowed. For several long, tender minutes, they clung together, enjoying the aftershocks.

He kissed the top of her head. "That was amazing," he said.

Her lips curved upward. "For me, too." She drew another deep satisfied breath. Shaking her head in mystification, she moved to look deep into his eyes. "I never imagined I could enjoy sex on a whim, just for pleasure. So this," she flattened her hand over his chest, confessing sincerely, "...this was a revelation."

To him, too.

He had married so young. For him sex, and love and commitment had always been inextricably combined. And once Shelby had passed, grief had shut down his desire. Until Tess had come into his life, anyway.

Unexpected hope rose. "Does this mean you're open to more?" he asked, before he could stop himself.

She bit her lip. Suddenly wavering. "This morning?"

God, he wanted to make love to her all over again. And again. He mimicked her almost too-casual tone. "Today. Whenever." He held her eyes, hoping she would give him the answer he needed and wanted to hear. So he could finally move past the ghost of Shelby, move on…to a full life. One that included more than just familial love.

Tess paused in uncertainty. Even before Noah's phone started buzzing.

The interruption was all they needed to bring them back to reality.

Tess extricated herself from him, the bliss from their lovemaking fading fast. He felt like they had gone from zero to sixty, and then back to zero again, landing with a grinding halt. Which wasn't surprising, given how high the barbed wire had been around her heart when they met. And to be fair, he'd had his share of reservations, about ever moving on, romantically, too.

"What's wrong?" he said. He knew she had enjoyed the interlude as much as he had. She had said so.

With an offhanded shrug, Tess looked around for her clothes. Emanating a nonchalant attitude, he sensed she didn't begin to feel, any more than he did right now, she flashed him a deadpan smile. "You mean besides the fact the morning is nearly gone, and I have to be at the clinic at noon?"

Knowing the key to not having this end here and

now was keeping this as informal as she seemed to need it to be, he caught her wrist and pulled her onto the bed, next to him. "Besides that."

She held her bundled clothes in front of her. Gazed down as if trying to figure out how to explain. "I thought I could handle a fling," she said mildly.

He sat quietly beside her, ignoring the instinctive need to haul her back in his arms and kiss her senseless. "And now?" he asked gently, sensing it would be a mistake to push her on this.

She raked her teeth across her lower lip. "It's just been a few minutes and I'm already second-guessing the wisdom of all this. Which is probably why—" Sobering slightly, she looked over at him. "Up to now, the only time I've been intimate with someone, we were in a committed relationship."

"Same here."

Swallowing, she continued, "Most of the time I'm too busy and frankly just not interested in even *going on a date*."

He had to ask. What had happened this morning? "So what's different now?"

You, he thought she was going to say. *Us*. But the moment passed. Her guard remained in place. She eased away from him slightly.

"Nothing, really. Which is why this can't happen again," she said.

Knowing it had to happen again, if they were ever going to take things to the next level, he let his gaze drift over her once again.

The question was...should he argue? Or be a gentleman and let her have her way?

Her voice quavered and he could see the uncertainty in her eyes. "I'm not an impulsive person, Noah. I can't let my emotions push me into doing things that aren't good for either of us in the long term."

Trying to hide his disappointment, he turned his back to let her dress, while he pulled on his boxer briefs and jeans. Shoving his arms through his shirt sleeves, he turned back to face her. Found her looking so damn sexy in her socks and undies. "What are you emotional about?"

She disappeared into the walk-in closet. "The stress of moving. Taking on a new job."

He sat down to put on his boots. "What else?"

She emerged in clinic scrubs. The stubborn set of her chin superseded the vulnerable sheen in her green eyes. "The house I inherited from Waylon." She offered a cordial smile. "I thought it would give me answers, and instead all it's done is present me with more questions."

He moved to help her make the bed. "Like?"

She shrugged, making no effort to mask her confusion. "Why was my mother so determined to leave Laramie when she was only eighteen? I mean, I get it. She didn't want to be a short-order cook in a small-town diner, like her mom. But to never come back, even after I was born...so she could introduce me to her mom before her mom passed. Why didn't she do that?" Tess asked, hurt vibrating in her low voice. "Why did my mother and grandmother remain estranged until my grandmother passed, of an undiagnosed heart ailment, when I was five?"

This time, Noah did take her in his arms. He pulled her comfortingly close. "Maybe they thought they still had time to work things out. That it would be easier for them if they waited."

Tess nodded, as if hoping that had been the situation.

Drawing a breath, she eased from his arms.

"In any case," he continued, consoling her the best way he knew how, "the house clearly meant something to Waylon. He might not have had a clue how to properly take care of it, but he came back to Laramie every chance he got. And then left that house to you. Probably because it *was* a link to the family."

"I know, right? He wanted me to have this tie to the past." Tess picked up a brush.

Knowing there was more, Noah waited.

She turned, her gaze locking intimately with his, then inhaled. "I thought by coming here and taking charge of the house that I would somehow feel closer to my mom, my grandfather and grandmother, and my uncle." She brushed her hair. "But they are as much strangers to me as they have always been."

"And that's frustrating."

A nod. "As well as disappointing."

Tess stepped in front of the mirror.

He lounged in the open doorway, watching her make up her face. "You don't have to keep the house. You could fix it up and sell it, or simply sell it as is, and buy another property here in Laramie. Start fresh."

Tess shook her head. She dropped her lipstick into her cosmetics bag. "That would feel disloyal. Even if it isn't giving me the connection to family that I had hoped it would."

He stepped back to let her pass. "Maybe that will come, when you renovate it and live there for a while. It's how it was here. I mean, I built the exact same house here we had in California for the girls and it still took months to feel like it was home."

"Really? The exact same house?"

"I didn't change a thing. Everything was exactly the way Shelby picked it out the first time. Right down to the tile." Too late, he realized this was probably not the time to be talking about his late wife. Not that Tess seemed to mind hearing about any of it.

She looked around admiringly. "Well, she had great taste, because your house is beautiful."

"Yeah." Noah exhaled in relief. "And it certainly made life easier for a time, because I had zero decisions to make when it came to overall design, materials, etc."

Brush still in hand, Tess glanced out the window. "What about the stable?" She swung back to him, curiosity lighting her eyes. "Did you have one in California, too?"

"No. Our house was in a small town outside of San Francisco. So, no one had any livestock. Or stables. Or paddocks."

Tess grinned, triumphant. "So, then, you did choose something."

"Not really. My dad helped me figure out all the specifications of that. Which I needed."

She picked up a hair clip from her bedside table. "Because your dad is a rancher?"

"Because the girls were having a hard time adjusting from the California lifestyle to the Texas."

She paused in surprise. "They really noticed the difference?"

"Well, not so much the twins, but Lucy? Yeah. She didn't understand why there were so many pick-up trucks on the road, or why everyone had a favorite pair of western boots. And it especially ticked her off that the tacos tasted weird to her."

Tess walked back over to the bathroom mirror. "Because California Mexican food is different than Tex-Mex. Or even Colorado Mexican."

"Right." He followed her lazily. "Plus, the weather was very different. It was really hot here that first summer. Lucy was used to a more mild climate, year round. Being able to go to the beach and take off her shoes and walk in the sand. Plus, we were just a couple of hours from the ski slopes, so we were able to take a couple of winter vacays she remembered, too."

"Let me guess." Tess frowned as she twisted her hair into a sleek knot, on the back of her head. "No snow here yet."

"Actually, last year there was a big ice storm, but the kids couldn't go out and play in it, so...no, that did not qualify in my girls' estimation."

Unhappy with the knot, which did seem to be listing slightly on one side, she released her curls, smoothed her hair with her fingertips, and began again. "Colorado has a lot of great skiing."

Noah caught her eyes in the mirror. "Do you know how?"

Her smile bloomed. "Oh yes. It was one of the first things I did when I got to college. Go on the school sponsored trips and learn to ski." She paused to look him over. "What about you?" she asked.

For reasons he didn't understand, he wanted to impress her. "Not black diamond, but yeah, I can ski."

Their glances meshed, held. For a moment he imagined what it would be like to take a trip like that with her.

Spectacular, probably.

It wasn't clear what she was thinking in that moment, but something positive…

Relieved the discomfiture that had followed their impulsive lovemaking had faded, he shrugged and said, "Something else we have in common then."

She secured her hair in place. Perfectly this time. "And that would be?" she matched his light, playful tone.

"A love of the winter vacay."

Tess sent him a rueful look before moving by him and disappearing into the closet again. Then she came out wearing the sneakers she wore to the clinic. "You know, cowboy, it would be a lot easier for me to keep my distance from you if you weren't so darn appealing."

He knew exactly what she meant.

"Right back at you, darlin'." He wanted to know so much more about her, too.

An awkward silence fell.

He moved forward and took her hands, loving the silky softness of her skin. "I have a proposal. We got off on the wrong foot. Mostly because once I saw you on Waylon's porch, ready to step into that mess, I couldn't mind my own business."

She gave him a look that said, *You think?*

"I had to try and rescue you."

Mischief twinkled in her eyes. "You do that a lot?"

"Never," he joked. "It gives women the wrong idea."

She smiled with wry humor.

Serious now, he went on with the recitation of his mistakes. Of which there were many. "Then we connected. And I got scared and I blew it. And put up all the wrong boundaries. Then I regretted it and couldn't stay away and now here we are."

"Here we are." Tess let out a tremulous breath.

With him hosting a woman in his home who wasn't his wife, an employee, or family member, and instead of being annoyed or indifferent, he was liking it. Way too much. Which was why he'd made love to her.

Her expression turned wary. "Not sure what to do next…" she murmured.

He thought about the advice his sister had given him the day before. Advice that had worked wonders for her and Cooper and their adopted triplets.

He took her hands in his. "How about we forget

all the previous stipulations we made and just take it one day, one *moment*, at a time?"

Tess regarded him cautiously. Tempted, yet... "I still don't want the girls hurt by any false assumptions on their part and I know you don't, either."

He shrugged. "So we'll keep things very light and casual and nonromantic around them."

"No long glances," she warned.

"Not a one," Noah promised, just as solemnly.

"Agreed," she said softly.

But even as he made this vow, Noah knew deep down it would be one that would be very hard to keep.

Chapter Eight

"Are you fighting?" Lucy asked Thursday evening, shortly after Tess came in from work.

Seven o'clock, and the girls were already in their pajamas. They were all sitting at the kitchen table, working on what appeared to be some sort of school project or homework, while Noah was rinsing the dinner dishes.

Noah and Tess turned to each other in surprise. They hadn't spent any time together since she'd left for work, the day before.

The time apart hadn't really eased the sexual sparks. She still felt them every time she looked his way. Which was why she was doing her best to be super casual, the way they had promised each other they would be, in the wake of their recent lovemaking.

Noah caught her eye, then turned back to Lucy. "Why would you think that, sweetheart?" he asked.

Lucy rested her chin on her upraised hand, still squinting at both of them. "Because you don't talk the way you usually do and you're not looking at each other. And when you and Mommy were mad at each other, she always gave you the silent treatment, so you didn't talk to her, either."

Wow, Tess thought. Nothing got by Noah's oldest daughter. She turned to face Lucy, too. "I'm not giving your dad the silent treatment, Lucy. I've just had two very long days at the vet clinic, and I guess I'm a little talked out."

"Are a lot of animals sick?" the eight-year-old asked in immediate concern.

Impressed by her empathy, Tess returned, "Some were. Others needed their yearly checkup or shots. And—" she paused for maximum dramatic effect "—there were a few really cute puppies, too."

The girls' eyes lit up. Tess pulled her phone from her pocket and brought up the clinic website's "Star Turn" page, where all the new pets photographs were. She walked over to show the girls, who oohed and aahed over each new pet.

"I wish I had your job," Lucy said.

"I want to grow lots of roses like Aunt Jillian," Avery interjected.

"Me, too," Angelica agreed dreamily.

"All good options," Noah said.

His phone buzzed. He checked caller ID. "I have to take this," he told them.

Lucy groaned. She buried her face in her hands. "Now I'll never get my practice spelling test done."

"We're making cards for our friend Danielle, who just had her tonsils out," Avery explained.

"So *we* can finish." Angelica colored all the more vigorously.

Tess made herself a cup of peppermint tea. Glad that she and Noah now had an agreement to take things one moment at a time, and would play it by ear, she took a seat at the table, too. Close by, Noah sat at his workstation and talked in serious tones. Clearly, this was a situation where he did need some assistance, if only for the length of the phone call.

"Can I help?" she asked Lucy.

"Do you know how to give a practice test?" the child asked warily.

Tess nodded.

Huffing out a breath, Lucy reluctantly handed over the words, her pencil poised over the blank page in front of her.

Tess asked her if she was ready to begin. She was. So Tess read the first word on the list. "Exercise."

Lucy sat there, staring at her. Perplexed at first, then clearly irritated.

Not sure she had pronounced it clearly, Tess said it again, as clearly as possible. "The first word on the list is *exercise*."

Lucy sighed and rolled her eyes, in full drama mode now. "Tess. You have to say it, and then use it in a sentence, and then repeat it, and then I write it down," she explained impatiently.

"Oh, right." Tess recalled her teachers doing just that. "Exercise," she said. "It's good for all adults and children to get exercise every day. Exercise…"

Satisfied, Lucy wrote her answer.

And so it went.

When they had finished all ten words, the twins were done with their get-well-soon cards, and Noah was off the phone. Lucy snatched up her paper. "You grade it, Daddy."

Noah looked it over. "Good job, Lucy. They're all correct."

Clearly not surprised she had aced it, Lucy glared at her dad and grumbled, "Tess makes up better sentences than you do."

Tess wasn't sure how to handle getting a compliment that also insulted someone else. Luckily, she didn't have to figure it out. Noah was shepherding the girls toward the stairs. Before they headed up for their bedtime routine, the twins dashed over to give Tess a good-night hug. Lucy offered only a beleaguered half smile and a sigh. "Thanks for helping me with my spelling test, Tess."

"You're welcome," she replied. Truth was, she had enjoyed it. Maybe too much.

After Noah and his daughters disappeared from view, Tess looked at Tank. He appeared as bonetired as she felt. The security monitor showed Miss Coco was still sleeping, just the way she had been when Tess had looked in on her when she got home.

She paused to pet the dog, then, her stomach

growling, she went to the fridge and got out one of the already prepared chicken Caesar salads she had picked up at the grocery store a few days earlier. She sat down at the island.

Noah came down the stairs. Looking *way* too good.

She watched as he strode into the kitchen and sat down on a stool beside her. He was wearing a business-casual shirt and slacks, which probably meant he'd had Zoom meetings and needed to dress accordingly. The sleeves were rolled up to his elbows, revealing sinewy forearms, with a dusting of dark hair. As always at this time of evening, he had damp splotches on his clothes and he smelled of kid shampoo and soap.

Which shouldn't have been all that sexy, but it was. She was beginning to realize she really liked seeing him in dad mode. It brought out a whole new side of him.

He rested his head on his elbow and looked over at her. "Guess you and I are going to need a new plan," he said, referring to the comments that had started off her evening, the moment she had returned to the ranch.

Wishing she could do what she really wanted to do, and take him by the hand and lead him right back up to her bed for another rollicking roll in the sheets, she worked off the clear plastic top on her store-bought salad. "Besides being super casual with each other?"

He held out a palm for her trash, then leaned over

to throw it away in the can. "Lucy is perceptive. She always has been."

Tess paused while she put the dressing over the top of the salad, then figured she had to ask. After all, if she and Noah were going to be friends, or even more than that, she had to know what she was getting into. She cut up her salad with a fork and knife. "It upset Lucy when you and Shelby argued?"

One corner of Noah's lip curled up. "Everything upsets Lucy one way or another, in case you didn't notice. But to answer your question, yes, she wanted absolute peace in the household one hundred percent of the time."

"And it wasn't that way?" she asked quietly.

Noah went back to the dinner dishes he'd abandoned. He took a moment to choose his words carefully. "Shelby and I were alike in that we each wanted what we wanted when we wanted it. When we were on the same page, that was great."

Tess could imagine.

He slid plates into the dishwasher, one by one. Then glasses and silverware. "When we weren't, it was problematic."

Tess continued to eat. "What did you fight about?" she asked, before she could stop herself.

Luckily, Noah didn't seem to mind.

He shrugged. "Early on, our quarrels were usually about how much time I was spending trying to get the business off the ground." His frown deepened. He got out the spray cleaner and some paper towels to clean the countertops, leaning over as he worked.

"Later, it was money...mostly." The muscles in his shoulders and arms bunched. "I wanted to put as much cash as possible back in the business, to keep growing it, and she wanted to enjoy the fruits of all my labor, ASAP. Which she did, when she wanted something specific, like a chocolate Lab puppy."

Tess looked down at Tank, who was curled at her feet. She mimed shock. "You didn't want this gorgeous fella?"

Seeming to know he was being talked about, he gazed up at her affectionately and thumped his tail.

Noah scoffed. Finished with the cleanup, he came back and settled beside her at the island. "Of course, I fell in love with him the moment I set eyes on him. The problem was, it wasn't a good time. She had just found out she was pregnant, and she already had Lucy to care for."

Which would have been a lot.

"I thought it was all going to be too much even before we found out she was having twins. But Lucy—who at four and a half wasn't thrilled about the idea of having to share the spotlight with two new siblings—was already incredibly emotionally attached to Tank. So he became a part of the family." Noah leaned over to pet the Lab.

Tess watched the free-flowing affection between the two. She speared another bite of the cold, delicious dinner salad. "It seems to have worked out."

Noah sobered. "Yeah, he was a huge comfort to Lucy when Shelby was diagnosed with breast cancer a few months after the twins were born and had to have a lumpectomy and then go through twelve weeks of chemotherapy."

"That must have been really hard."

"It was. And before you ask, no, I did not deny Shelby *anything* after that. No matter what the ask." His tone turned gravelly. Eyes glistening, he glanced away. "I just wanted her to stay with us."

Tess realized she didn't know how he had lost his wife. "So what happened?" she asked gently, touching his arm. "Did the cancer come back?"

Noah shook his head. "No, she was in remission when she died."

"Then…?" Sensing her touch wasn't helping, Tess dropped her hand and sat back.

"It was an accident." His lips compressed into a thin line. "Shelby was trying to get her strength back and she went out running every morning with her friends, and she tripped and fell and struck her head on the curb. She was gone by the time the paramedics got her to the hospital."

"Oh, Noah…"

Head bent forward, almost as if in prayer, he clasped his hands tightly in front of him. "After that, all I could think of was the time we had wasted, not getting along, or just appreciating every moment for the gift it was, you know…?"

"I do. I felt the same way when I lost my mom."

Another silence fell. This time it was one of remembered grief, intimacy and connection.

Noah cleared his throat, looking ready to move on. "Anyway, sorry about Lucy jumping to conclusions earlier, about us being angry with each other," he told her sincerely. "I know it made you uncomfortable."

"She was right to speak up if something was on her mind."

He studied her, his heart suddenly on his sleeve. "I'm glad you feel that way, too," he said softly.

Yet another connection that was forging between them.

She wasn't sure what any of this meant, if anything. So the logical thing to do was ask. She rested her chin on her upraised fist, hoping what had happened between them before wasn't just a winter fling, that their newfound camaraderie wouldn't fade away. Summoning her courage, she did her best to pretend an insouciance she couldn't really begin to feel.

"So, um, Noah?"

"Yeah?" he asked, waiting patiently for her to continue.

"Do you think it would be okay if the kids knew I was becoming a family friend of you-all?" she asked before she could stop herself.

Clearly, they were going to have to tell them something. Especially Lucy.

"Absolutely, we should mention that." Desire that matched her own flared in his eyes. He sat back in his chair, his broad shoulders flexing against the starched fabric of his dress shirt. Gruffly, he continued, "As well as good friends to each other."

Good friends.

She realized that was not quite what she wanted, but it would do for now.

* * *

Tess worked late again Friday evening, delivering a Shetland pony on the other side of the county. By the time she got back to the Welcome Ranch around midnight, everyone but Noah was fast asleep.

He heated up a dinner plate of leftover lasagna for her, and they shared a glass of wine and talked about their days while she ate.

"I think Lucy actually missed you this evening," Noah confided.

Tess thought about the hot-and-cold reception she often got from his eldest daughter. Wanting to believe they were getting closer, she regarded him hopefully. She needed to know what lay ahead. Would their passion remain a one-off? Or build into something stronger? She knew for certain he and his girls were a package deal. As they should be.

So for anything real or lasting to happen between the two of them, all three of his daughters would have to be fully on board.

Tess sipped her wine. "You're not just saying that?" she asked anxiously.

His smile reached his eyes. He leaned in close, inundating her with the brisk, woodsy scent of his cologne and the deeper, inherently masculine fragrance of his skin. He traced the inside of her wrist with the tip of his index finger. "She wanted you to know she got a one hundred on her spelling test."

Tingles spread outward, moving up her arm to the center of her chest. Heat gathered low in Tess's middle. Wishing they could make love, yet knowing they wouldn't—not here, not now, with his kids in the house—she contented herself with the fact he had waited up for her, so they could spend this time alone together. "I have a feeling she gets one hundreds quite frequently."

"True." He drew back just far enough to peer into her eyes. "But this time she credited you and your help."

They exchanged happy grins.

"The twins wanted to see you, too."

Aware she hadn't been this relaxed or felt this free in a long time, she surveyed him, too, drinking in his handsome features and the scruff of beard on his jaw. Heart skittering in her chest, she asked, "You're not worried about them getting too used to having me around?" she asked quietly, aware she was on the verge of a happiness and a sense of belonging unlike anything she had ever felt before.

"Not anymore." Noah leaned closer and this time his lips did brush her brow. Briefly, he held her close. "Not when your presence is bringing us all so much joy."

"Daddy, did you ask Tess yet?" Lucy asked pointedly as Tess was getting ready to go to work Saturday morning.

"Ask me what?" She finished filling her travel mug with fresh, hot coffee.

"To go to dinner tonight at the Circle L!" Avery said.

"All the cousins get to play while the moms have

a bake-a-thon with Gramma this afternoon and then we're all going to eat dinner together!" Angelica explained.

Already starting to feel a little overwhelmed, like this was a test she most definitely did not want to fail, Tess asked, "What time does it start?"

Noah joined her next to the coffee maker. "Around midafternoon. My siblings and their spouses will start showing up when their little ones wake up from their naps."

Things were moving both too fast and too slow with her and Noah. She wanted to know a lot more about him. Yet, at the same time, she wasn't sure she was ready to go to a big family dinner with him, where she was most likely going to be the only newbie. Even though she had briefly met a lot of the Lockharts before, when they had helped her clear out her house, it seemed like a lot of pressure.

Especially for someone like her, who had grown up an only child of a single mom.

"Hmm." Tess eased on her coat, trying to figure out if she should delay this kind of gathering until she at least knew Noah and his girls a lot better. "Can I let you know when I get done at the clinic?"

Noah's regard remained maddeningly inscrutable. "Sure. No pressure."

Appeased, she said goodbye to the girls, who were already headed off to the playroom upstairs.

Noah walked her as far as the door. Then grabbed his coat and whistled for Tank. "Need to go out, buddy?"

Tail wagging, the chocolate Lab followed them outside.

Noah fell into step beside her, keeping an appropriate distance, in case Lucy was watching from an upstairs window. Which, as it turned out, the little sleuth was. Hands shoved in the pockets of his jacket, he remained several feet away and watched as she put her vet bag and thermos in the Tahoe. With a casual grin, he asked, "Anything I can say to convince you it'd be a *great* idea for you to join us at my folks' today?"

Wow, he had a one-track mind. When he wanted something, he went right after it.

Tess paused, her hand on the car door. "Not sure." This was the second invitation she had fielded from Carol and Robert Lockhart in a week. She swallowed around the dryness of her throat. "Will your parents keep asking until I go?"

Mischief lit his eyes. "Most likely."

So then, how to mitigate any potential faux pas? She squinted at him thoughtfully. "Could I just show up in time for dinner? And not participate in the bake-a-thon?"

He exhaled, evidently still playing it casual. "If you want to avoid disappointing the ladies, probably not."

He caught her confused look, then explained, "My sister Jillian was here earlier in the week and had one of the scones you made. She hasn't stopped raving about it."

"Oh." That was nice, wasn't it?

"The ladies were all hoping you would share some

tips with them. Unless—" he paused to give her a lazy once-over that set her to tingling anew "—you are one of those people who keep their recipes secret?"

She scoffed at the ridiculousness of the idea. "No, of course not." Food was for sharing and bringing people together, not driving them apart!

His dark eyebrows lifted. "Then…?"

Realizing she needed all the protection she could get, she said, "Will everyone be aware I'm just coming as your friend?"

From his immediate response, she could tell that he not only got her resistance to romantic meddling, but also shared it. "And temporary houseguest. You bet." He waited until she got in her vehicle. "I'll send out a group text and make sure that is crystal clear to them." He shut the driver door for her.

Which meant it would all be fine, Tess thought with a measure of relief, as she drove away from him. Wouldn't it?

Chapter Nine

Tess was barely in the Circle L ranch-house door before she was surrounded by a group of female family members. Thanks to the way they had all pitched in during the marathon clean-out of her home, she knew all but one.

The effervescent blonde radiated warmth and sophistication. "Hi, Tess."

Before she could do more than draw a breath, she was enveloped in an easy hug that spoke volumes about the generosity and warmth of the Lockhart clan.

Drawing back, her host said, "I'm Mackenzie, Noah's sister from Fort Worth."

"The one who's married to Griff and has twin toddlers, Jenny and Jake? And a Bernese mountain dog named Bliss?"

"Right. Wow...you must have a great memory."

About pets and their owners, yes, she did. "Noah was updating me on the way over," she explained.

Mackenzie shot an affectionate glance at her brother, who was engulfed in his own series of greetings and hugs.

More followed for Tess, too.

"Sounds just like him," Mackenzie said affectionately.

Finally, she was escorted to the big, homey ranch-house kitchen, where over a half a dozen baking stations were already set up.

"Ready to part with all your scone-making secrets?" Noah's sister Faith asked with a smile. Newly married to her adopted son's biological father, she radiated joy.

"I am." Tess put on the apron handed to her. "I just hope I don't disappoint."

Fortunately, her audience was as patient as they were serious about learning all the tricks her professional chef mother had taught her. From using supercold shaved butter and heavy cream to not over-mixing the dough.

Each woman added a different ingredient to their concoction, everything from chopped fresh fruit to nuts and dark chocolate. When all the scones were rotating in and out of Carol's two large wall ovens, the women worked together to clean up.

And that was, of course, when the questions started.

"Was it hard for you leaving Denver?" Faith queried.

"You grew up and went to school there, right?" Gabe's wife, Susannah, asked right after.

"Yes. My first thirty years were all spent in Colorado. I grew up in Denver, went to Colorado State University for undergrad and vet school. That's in Fort Collins. And then I moved back to the Denver area, for my first job as a veterinarian."

"Did you relocate here just because of the house you inherited from Waylon?" Jillian asked.

Carol sent her daughter a look, seeming to warn her not to be too nosy. Even if she was Noah's closest female sibling.

"Or were you looking for adventure or even a fresh start?" Cade's wife, Allison, asked.

Probably trying to help divert attention away from Noah, Tess thought. Because, surely, those inquiries were coming soon. Tess sent Allison—who had already helped her find married local contractors Molly and Chance to do her house renovation—a grateful glance. "I've always been interested in Texas. And wanted to know more about my family who lived here."

Noah's mother cleared her throat.

Mackenzie shrugged. "Maybe she has someone special set to join her soon."

Everyone turned in curiosity. Tess felt herself flush, not sure what to say. "I, uh, was in a long-term relationship until a couple of years ago. Since, I've concentrated on my career."

"So you're open to someone new?" Travis's wife, Skye, a registered nurse, asked. "Because it's never good to spend too long alone…"

* * *

The kids were bursting with energy, and the day was sunny and clear, so Noah and the rest of the men took them all outside to play in the big, fenced backyard, which had a playset and a sandbox. While they stood around and supervised the children, there was a lot of guy talk. First, predictions about the current football playoffs and upcoming Super Bowl. College basketball and the ever-popular March Madness was next. Then cattle. Horses. Schools. And finally, the latest "romance" in the family.

Gabe, the oldest, asked, "Is Tess your date?"

Yes, Noah thought, but remembering his promise to her, he said, "No."

Mackenzie's husband, Griff, an attorney never shy about giving advice, said, "Well, she should be."

His retired professional-baseball-playing brother, the former ladies' man of the bunch, elbowed him in the side. "You snooze, you lose," Cade teased.

The idea that he would let any guy cut in line ahead of him rankled. Noah turned, and reminded Cade, "Hey. She's living with me." What would they call that? If not getting his bid for attention in. And staking his claim. Every. Single. Day.

Eyebrows raised all around.

Noah bit down on a curse.

Damn, he was rusty with all this.

He'd really forgotten the finer points of dating a woman. If he had ever really known them, that was. Since he had gone straight from high school to freshman year of college to marriage.

Aware he was getting that look—the one that said he needed to up his game—Noah cleared his throat and tried again. "I mean staying with me," he corrected with as much gentlemanly ease as possible. "Temporarily."

Travis, the most recently married, chuckled. He rubbed a hand across his jaw. "Yeah, and I bet you wish those repairs on her house will never get done."

Actually, Noah thought, there was some truth to that. He liked sharing space with her. Trading confidences. Making love...

"Speaking of Tess..." his dad interrupted kindly. He inclined his head in the direction of the kitchen's big bay window. "Don't look now, but looks like she's getting the third degree."

Noah glanced over. The women were gathered around Tess, the way the guys had just been gathered around him. And his gut told him it wasn't because they were currently having a cooking lesson. He grimaced. He had promised Tess this wouldn't happen. "Excuse me." He turned on his heel. "I've got a rescue to undertake."

He slipped in the back door. Then sauntered into the kitchen, cheerfully disrupting whatever conversation had been going on.

Tess remained where she was, giving him a mild look. But he could feel her gratitude surging in his direction.

To make sure it didn't happen again, he stayed close by her the rest of the day. And begged off early, after dinner, to go back to Welcome Ranch to check on Miss Coco. They took the girls down to the barn with them.

Tess opened up her vet bag and examined the pregnant jennet while the girls watched. "Is she going to have her baby soon?" Lucy asked.

"I think it's still going to be at least another week," Tess replied, palpitating the donkey's midsection and checking out the position of the foal.

"How will you know for sure?" Angelica murmured curiously, hunkering down next to Tess. Her twin did the same.

Noah kneeled, too. Wanting to make sure that Tess had enough room to maneuver, he brought both twins onto his lap, while Lucy hung back a little, watching.

"Because Miss Coco will know her baby is ready to come out, and she'll let me know," Tess explained. She gave Noah a look, as if hoping the girls didn't need more specific information.

But he knew if they did, and he gave permission, which he would, that she would answer their questions as kindly and carefully as possible, making sure not to upset them.

Luckily, they took the lack of absolute due date in stride. Probably because they had already been waiting months for the foal to arrive.

Avery turned to Noah. "Daddy, after this baby is born, will Miss Coco have another foal?"

Another? Noah's brow furrowed. He wasn't sure what she was trying to ask. "You mean like twins?"

"No," Angelica inserted, picking up where her twin sister left off. "Like next year."

Thank heaven they had no male donkeys around. Noah shook his head, sure about this much. "No. Two donkeys is enough for us," he said.

Angelica looked at Tess. "What about you?" Noah's three-year-old asked. "Do *you* have any babies?"

Tess had thought the inquisition from Noah's sisters was intrusive, in that well-meant, protective family way. But she hadn't expected *this*.

Trying not to wonder what Noah thought about her having a baby—with anyone—she smiled and said, "No, I don't, honey."

Lucy finally moved away from the stall door. Arms folded in front of her, she stared Tess down. "Do you want some?"

Did she?

Up to now, she had pretty much ruled it out. Mainly because she didn't want to parent alone, while juggling a demanding career and being sole financial support of the family, the way her mom had.

But now, being around Noah and his kids and his big, extended family, she was beginning to see it as a real possibility. Even if the only man she could currently see taking on the starring role in her daydream was the man opposite her. The man who had vowed never to marry again.

She supposed that also meant never having any more kids.

And that would be disappointing, she realized without warning. Gut-wrenchingly so.

Aware everyone was still waiting for her answer, she said, "Maybe someday. But I'd need to get married first. Now—" she put one earpiece of her stethoscope in her ear and held out the other for a willing volunteer "—who else wants to hear Miss Coco's heartbeat?"

An hour later, Tess was sitting on the porch steps, watching Tank explore the yard, when the front door eased open and then quietly closed.

Noah sat down beside her, his thigh touching hers. "I'm aware you have every right to be irritated with me."

It helped, knowing he was sensitive to how difficult that Lockhart family shindig had been for her. She leaned into his touch for one millisecond before pulling away. "Your sisters were just being protective. Your mother tried to stop them."

"To no avail, apparently."

His droll tone brought a rueful smile to her face. She turned to face him. As their eyes met and held, she felt a shimmer of tension arc between them.

Man-woman tension.

Doing her best to maintain a poker face, Tess shrugged. "Lockharts are stubborn, when they get on a mission, I'm beginning to see."

He reached up and tucked a strand of hair behind her ear. "No kidding. But don't discount my mother. She's matchmaking, too."

Tess bit her lip. "Hence the two dinner invitations in one week." Only one of which had been accepted. Would today have been less stressful if she had gone to his folks' home both times?

Tess was unable to say.

Noticing she was shivering in a too-light fleece, Noah took off his jacket and draped it over her shoulders. Just like that, she was inundated with the warmth of his body and the woodsy scent of his cologne.

He leaned closer, whispering in her ear. "Well, she *is* a social worker…"

"And she thinks I need…work?" Tess said, unable to hold back the quip.

He laughed and shook his head. "No. But she does think a closed heart can get stuck shut."

Interesting. Tess snuggled deeper into the warmth of his coat. "Hmm." It was so nice on the porch steps, with the velvety black sky overhead, sprinkled with stars and a golden quarter moon. They were both going to be too cold sitting out here. She knew that. Yet, she wasn't quite ready to leave the peace and quiet of a Texas night in January.

Figuring the least she could do was share a little body heat, Tess scooted a little closer, until they were touching from hip to ankle, shoulder to waist. She gazed out over the ranch. Thinking *Welcome* was exactly the right name. She certainly felt at home here.

She just hoped her heart didn't get stuck shut. The way Carol Lockhart seemed to fear…

"Maybe that's what happened to my mom and grandmother." With a shrug, Tess mused quietly,

"They walled off their feelings for each other, and then didn't know how to open up to each other once again."

He caught her hand in his and clasped it tightly. "I'm sorry about that."

She pulled their entwined fingers onto her lap. "Me, too. But it's in the past, and nothing can be done about it now, so—" she squared her shoulders and sat up straighter "—I need to stop dwelling on it, and move forward."

With a sexy half smile, he regarded her with admiration. "To...?"

"Getting a family like yours. And all the ones your siblings and parents enjoy."

That was ultimately what was going to make her happy. She knew that now. She wanted someone to share life's ups and downs with.

He continued holding her hand. "You mean that?"

Aware he was truly trying to understand her, she drew a breath. "I do."

As their eyes met, and held, she felt warmed through and through. "The thing is," he said softly, "we've got time to figure this out."

That's what Carlton had said, from the time they started dating, until they broke up: *We don't have to rush into anything...*

But Noah wasn't her ex.

He understood there was more to life than ambition, goals and a successful career.

He also seemed to appreciate the importance of sharing one's thoughts and feelings. Shaking his head ruefully, he continued, "Maybe it's because of the way my birth parents died, so suddenly, but it seems like I've been in a hurry my whole life. With Shelby. My work. I even tried to rush through the grieving process, after Shelby passed."

"Did that work for you?" Tess couldn't help but ask.

He paused, considering. "Yes and no. I mean I know I will always be sad about the loss, but I realize now that I am ready to move on, too."

Joy unfurled slowly inside Tess.

She was ready to embrace a new future, too.

"Which is why," Noah continued sincerely, squeezing her hand in his, "for the first time, I want to slow down and really enjoy each moment of my life. Take my time, getting to know you. See where whatever this is between us is going to take us."

Tess knew what a huge admission this was for him. "I'd like to get to know you a whole lot better, too," she said quietly. Except she wanted to do it a whole lot *faster*. Which was ironic, because for the first time in her life, she found herself wanting to not be as incredibly patient as she had been taught to be for so many years, but to rush in where fools feared to tread.

Who would have figured that?

Chapter Ten

"So what do you think?" Molly asked Tess, during their midjob walk-through Tuesday evening, after she'd finished work at the clinic.

Tess gazed at the interior of her home, in wonder. Joy flowed through her. "I can't believe you've only been working on this renovation for nine days!"

Molly grinned. "Chance and I told you we'd get it done on time."

They had definitely said that.

And right now, Tess believed they would. The mess of a house she'd inherited was no longer visible. A light neutral color adorned all the walls. The plumbing and electric had been redone, the new HVAC keeping the interior cozy, and a gas fireplace insert had been installed.

True, the newly sanded wood floors still needed

to be stained and sealed, the bathroom upstairs finished and a new half bath put in the first floor, next to the expanded laundry room.

But recessed lighting throughout the first floor made it bright and cheerful against the wintry darkness outside.

Molly walked with Tess back into the kitchen, which remained a blank slate. She spread the plans for the kitchen across a piece of plywood on two sawhorses. Then opened up the folder that held the materials that would be used to finish it out. Creamy ivory cabinets, a farmhouse sink. Room for a French door refrigerator/freezer and dishwasher. Molly sobered. "I want to make sure you want a four-burner gas stove, not an ultradeluxe chef's model."

Tess shot her a curious look.

The contractor explained, "Word of your culinary talent is getting out, among the community. So I wanted to make sure you would be happy with the standard model you picked out."

Ah...small towns. Where everyone knew everyone. Pleased to have Molly watching out for her, too, Tess said, "My mom definitely would have gone for the higher-end model, with the six burners, center griddle and double ovens. As an executive chef, she wouldn't have been happy with anything less. But honestly, I only cook for myself, and that's when I'm off."

The other woman nodded, listening intently, giving her all the time she needed to consider.

Tess told herself not to second-guess her decision.

"If I had a family—" like Noah and the girls "—it would be different, of course."

Molly's expression gentled. "You don't think that will happen?"

It hadn't yet.

And wishes weren't reality.

Better not to talk about what she was beginning to want in the worst way. For the first time in her life.

Tess exhaled. "No."

Molly's face lit up. An intuitive woman, she touched Tess's arm empathetically. "That's what I said before Chance and I got together. And look at us now. Happily married parents to two! So you never know..."

No, you didn't. Although Tess had been working hard to keep from thinking too far ahead. Yes, she and Noah and the girls were getting along splendidly, and she felt more at home with them every day. Noah had kept to his promise from the previous week, about going slow.

While she privately kept yearning for more.

Which wasn't good, she knew.

Especially if it turned out their friendship/one-time fling was one based in convenience. Nothing deeper...

Molly asked a few more questions regarding the quartz countertops and backsplash, the size of the island she was going to put in. "When do you expect your belongings to get here?" she asked.

Tess hesitated. "I'm not sure. Everything is still in storage. I have to let the movers know when I want them to get it on the truck. Once I do, they said it would take a couple of weeks to get it here."

"You probably should do that now, then," Molly said.

"I will," Tess promised.

Excitement flooded through her. It was *happening*. She was finally going to have a home of her own, renovated exactly to her specifications. Whatever else happened, she could be happy about that.

Molly gathered up the samples. "Well, I need to get home for dinner," she said.

"I need to get going, too," Tess murmured. She needed to check on Miss Coco. Plus, Noah or the girls might need help with something.

They walked around, turning off the interior lights.

"How is it going at the Welcome Ranch?" Molly asked.

Good question. One she was going to have difficulty answering candidly. "Mmm… Noah's been great. Very kind."

Molly paused to slip on her coat. "How about Lucy and the twins?"

"I'm half family friend, half houseguest to them. So they don't want to eat dinner without me, because 'that is rude if you are having guests.' But they also know there are times when I have to work late, or go out on a house or ranch call, before I head 'home' for the night, so…"

"Yeah, I can see how that could feel a little awkward at times."

Awkward and too cozy and a legion of other things…

Tess checked her phone to make sure there were

no messages, then put on her coat, too. "Anyway, when I can, I try to do dishes or help with dinner or fold laundry as a way to repay Noah for putting me up."

Molly smiled in understanding. "I'm sure he appreciates whatever you do. I was a single parent to one, until Braden was almost five, and it was hard. I can't imagine how Noah has managed with three…"

Admirably well, Tess thought. She had no doubt he would go back to coping on his own just fine. It was herself, going back to a life alone, she was beginning to worry about.

"How did the walk-through go?" Noah asked Tess, twenty minutes later.

"Fine." Vet bag in hand, she strode into the stable, where it seemed his entire family was gathered. Including their chocolate Labrador retriever, Tank. "What's going on?"

"We can't get Tank to come back to the house," Avery explained.

"And we don't know why he doesn't want to come with us," Lucy said, looking upset. "He *always* comes when it's about dinnertime."

"Maybe he's just not hungry," Angelica mused.

Tess could see Tank hanging out in the aisleway, in the middle of the barn, across from Miss Coco's stall.

"He's been like this all day," Noah said. "Every time I let him out he makes a beeline for the stable. And won't leave until he goes inside and checks on

Miss Coco. I have to snap a leash on him to get him to go back to the house."

Tess walked over to Tank and petted him on the head. "Sounds like you're doing a great job of guarding today, buddy."

She opened the wooden half door and went in to see the miniature donkey. Swiftly spotting the reason, she looked at Noah. "The foal is starting to turn." Which was one of the first signs of impending birth.

"What is that?" Lucy asked curiously.

Noah gave a barely perceptible nod, letting her know it was okay to continue.

Tess surveyed the girls gently, making eye contact with each. "Miss Coco is getting ready to have her baby donkey."

"Now?" Angelica and Avery clapped their hands and jumped up and down excitedly, squealing.

Noah put his finger to his lips. "Shhh!" He whispered sternly, "You don't want to scare our pets."

They settled immediately, somewhat chagrined. "Sorry, Daddy," the twins murmured in unison.

"It takes a while for the mama donkey to get ready to give birth, so it's not going to happen right away," Tess cautioned.

"When do you think?" His handsome face etched with concern, Noah echoed his eldest daughter's query.

Once again, she tried not to think how intimate this all felt. "Maybe by the weekend."

Lucy crossed her arms. Recalcitrant once again. "That can't happen. We are going to Fort Worth to see Aunt Mackenzie and Uncle Griff and *their* twins, with all the rest of our cousins." Hands on her hips, she swung back to Noah. "Daddy, tell Tess to tell Miss Coco she has to wait!"

Noah put a gentle hand on her shoulder. He looked down at her, and patiently soothed, "It doesn't work that way, honey."

Lucy became even more defiant. She stomped her rubber-boot-clad foot. "But I want to see the baby donkey be born!"

"So do I!" chimed the twins, continuing to squeal loudly in excitement.

Noah shushed them all once again. "That's not a good idea."

Lucy's lower lip trembled. "Why not?" she demanded.

Sensing it was time for a little medical expertise, Tess interjected, "Because it is a very private and special time for a mama donkey, and she needs to have quiet, so she can't have a lot of people around while she is trying to give birth. It's too distracting. And it makes her very nervous and unhappy during what should be a very special, joyful time for her and her new foal."

Lucy considered that, her inherent kindness coming to the fore once again. "Are you going to be there?" she asked Tess.

Happy to see Noah's eldest was calm again, she replied, "Yes."

"Are you?" Lucy's eyes swung toward her dad.

"Yes, I am," he said.

"Then I want to be there, too," the eight-year-old insisted.

Noah frowned. "Even if it makes it harder for Miss Coco and her new baby donkey?" he returned.

Lucy fell silent. Torn between what she selfishly wanted, and what she knew was right.

"How about this?" Tess intervened gently once again. "How about your dad and I make a video of it, so we can show you later."

That had all three girls' attention—and approval.

"Can I see the baby donkey after it is born?" Lucy asked.

"Absolutely," Tess said while, beside her, Noah nodded his consent, too. She looked his oldest daughter in the eye. "I will introduce you and your sisters to the new foal. We'll do it one person at a time, so Miss Coco and her baby won't feel overwhelmed. And I will teach you how to touch them and talk to them, and care for them, too." Because imprint training should include the entire family to be truly successful.

Lucy exhaled in satisfaction. "Okay," she said, finally relenting. "But Miss Coco still has to wait until we get back from Fort Worth. Do you hear that, Miss Coco?" she scolded affectionately, before she left, giving their pet donkey a final loving stroke across her brow. "You need to wait to have your foal, until we get back on Sunday!"

"Are you going to Fort Worth with the girls?" Tess asked later that evening, after the kids were all asleep.

Noah set down an armload of firewood, next to the hearth.

His shoulders flexed as he shrugged out of his winter jacket and went to hang it up. "Normally, yes, I would." He walked back, his strides purposeful. Slanting her a glance over his shoulder, he added in a low, reassuring tone that sent tingles pouring through her, "But not with Miss Coco about to deliver."

Tess settled on the sofa with a basket of mismatched children's socks she had offered to sort. Anything to keep her hands and mind busy. And off the building desire to be intimate with him again.

She swallowed around the tightness in her throat. "I could get some help from the vet clinic if you like."

Noah hunkered down to build the fire. Denim stretched across his muscular legs and butt. Her body heated in response. "No. I want to be here." He reached to the left, and the same thing happened with the fabric of his shirt. It molded to his buff upper body and strong arms, reminding Tess what a fine body he had. "And, by the way, thanks for helping explain to the girls why they can't witness the birth."

She found two pink-and-white polka-dot wool socks and rolled them into a ball. "I agree with you. It'd be a bad idea."

Noah frowned over at her. "You say that like you're speaking from experience."

Tess nodded, deciding to be forthright, so he would know in advance what a worst-case scenario could look like. "When I was working at my previous job, I had a family that wanted to watch the birth of their miniature donkey's foal. The kids were all pretty young. I worried they would be too excited or maybe even scared by what they were going to see but—" she inhaled deeply, forcing herself to go on "—I was overruled."

Noah stuffed paper into the open spaces in the set logs. He sat back and reached for the long matches. "What happened?"

Tess shut her eyes briefly and continued sorrowfully. "There was a complication." She forced herself to meet Noah's eyes. Watched while he lit the fire, then rose and came back to sit beside her. "The foal came out with the cord wrapped around her neck."

He settled nearer, draping an arm along the back of the sofa, close enough to warm her shoulders. "Oh, no."

Horrifyingly, yes. "The parents saw and became hysterical that we were going to lose the foal. The kids followed suit." Tess shook her head, recalling the crying and screaming and panicked shouting. "I got everyone out of the way and saved both jennet and foal, but needless to say, there were some really tense moments."

He drew her closer still. "I can imagine."

"The kids were traumatized to the point the vet clinic waived the family's entire bill and I had to apologize to them. The thing was—" she paused to lick her lips "—I knew it was a bad idea, but I had no say."

His gaze roved her face. Commiserating. "Now you do?"

"Oh, yes, I made sure of that before I signed on with the clinic here."

He was looking at her like he wanted to kiss her again. But she knew if they started, they wouldn't want to stop. And with the kids right upstairs... It made more sense to wait until the next morning, when the girls were at school, and she didn't have to be at work until noon.

The unmasked longing in his eyes indicated he was thinking the same thing.

He touched a strand of her hair, rubbing it between his fingertips. "So..." He waggled his eyebrows at her, letting her know he still yearned to be with her as much as she yearned to be with him. "If you decided to kick me out of the stable when it's time...?"

"I could."

Their gazes meshed. Lingered. They exchanged knowing smiles.

Without warning, Tess knew morning couldn't come soon enough. "But I won't. We had a deal, remember?" She bent her head and went back to sorting socks. "I'm going to teach you how to imprint-train your family's new foal." With a flirtatious gaze aimed back at him, she murmured, "Plus, having grown up on a ranch, I imagine you saw this kind of thing all the time."

His sensual lips curved into an inviting smile. "I did. I even helped out a time or two." He suddenly sobered. "But I feel like this is going to be *different*."

Tess thought so, too.

Part of it was professional pride. She wanted things

to go smoothly. The rest had to do with the time she and Noah would spend together, bringing new life into the world, helping the baby donkey draw his or her first breath. It was the kind of intimate activity that would bring them closer.

But was it the kind of closeness that would endure?

Only time would give her the answer to that.

Chapter Eleven

"No school today?" Tess remarked in surprise on Friday morning. She was usually the first out the door during the weekdays, with Noah following an hour later, girls in tow. However, this morning, the three girls were already dressed in matching pink cords and sweaters. Their wheeled suitcases were next to the front door, along with their backpacks.

"It's a teacher workday, so we get the day off!" Lucy said importantly.

"Which is why we get to go to Fort Worth with Gramma and Grandpa early!" Avery announced.

"Ah." Tess grinned. "Now it all makes sense." She'd thought the girls were leaving at the end of the day. Not the beginning.

"We get to go to the zoo this afternoon," Angelica added.

"And the science museum tomorrow." Avery handed Tess a hairbrush. "Can you put my hair in a ponytail?" She had an elastic around her wrist.

"Sure." Tess smiled.

"Mine, too," Angelica said.

Tess fixed both girls hair. Lucy had done her own ponytail, but now she undid it. And walked over silently to Tess, handing over her elastic.

Happy to be included, Tess did as asked, while Noah watched silently, a quietly affectionate look on his face.

She understood the depth of his emotion.

She was falling in love with his kids, too.

"Can we go down and say goodbye to Miss Coco before we leave?" Lucy asked.

"Sure." Noah handed out coats. Together, they walked outside and trooped across the lawn, Tank beside them.

Miss Coco was sitting half-upright when they walked in, panting slightly. Her belly was protruding more than ever. "Do you think she's uncomfortable?" Lucy asked Tess worriedly. Tenderly, she stroked her pet's head.

"Yes. But most mamas are when they get to the end stages of their pregnancy," Tess said. "But not to worry. I think Miss Coco knows that is a good thing. It means her baby foal is getting ready to be born."

"But not 'til we get back from Aunt Mackenzie and Uncle Griff's house, right, Daddy?" Angelica reminded him.

Avery kneeled down to stroke Miss Coco'a soft brown tail. "We want to be here with her."

"I am sure Miss Coco knows how you feel," Noah said gently.

The sound of a vehicle approaching had him going to the door. "Kids, say goodbye now. Your ride is here!"

They scrambled to get ready. In their excitement, they embraced their dad and then impulsively stopped to give Tess hugs, too.

She held each of the girls in turn. Aware all over again how wonderful it would be to have a family like this, of her own. Or even to remain part of this one, in some way...

Tess walked to the door, waving at Carol and Robert. She turned to Noah. "I've got a few things I want to check out."

"No problem. I'll see them off and be right back."

When he returned, Tess was kneeling in the straw next to Miss Coco, who had decided to lie down again.

"More signs?" Noah asked.

Tess nodded, showing him. "The teats are all the way enlarged and they've developed a waxy cap on the ends." Tess ran her hands over the top of the jennet's body. "See these grooves on either side of Miss Coco's spine, near the tail? That means her pelvic ligaments are softening in preparation. Plus, the area around the opening of her birth canal is elongated and loose and soft."

"So... Soon?"

"I'm thinking maybe late tonight."

Briefly, Noah looked a little panicked. "What should I do?"

"Just keep an eye on her through the security camera. Check on her every hour or so. And let me know if she gets restless."

Tess could see he was still anxious. The way she would be if she was in his position. She sent him a reassuring smile. "I can be here in fifteen minutes, if you need me. All you have to do is call or text. I'm seeing patients at the clinic, but I'll have my phone on me all day."

Noah turned to the pregnant jennet. He kneeled down beside her and stroked her head gently, looking deep into the miniature donkey's soft, dark eyes. "You hear that, Miss Coco? There's nothing for you to worry about. You're not going through this alone. Tess and I will both be here," he promised.

Noah sent Tess updates through the day, brief texts that indicated what she expected to hear...that everything was the same.

She was just walking out to her Tahoe when the phone rang. She glanced at the caller ID. Instantly alert. "Noah?"

"All of a sudden, she's really restless," he informed her gravely. "I think it's time."

"Hang on. I'll be right there," Tess promised. "And, in the meantime, maybe you should set up the video camera so we can edit a movie of the birth for the kids."

"Already done."

"Great. See you shortly."

The drive went quickly.

Instead of parking next to the house and walking down, she left her SUV next to the stable and headed in. Noah was standing in the aisleway, arms crossed, concern etching deep grooves in his handsome face. She joined him where he stood.

"See that?" He pointed to Miss Coco's swollen genitals, flush with the hindquarters.

"Definitely getting ready to give birth," Tess said, glad he had called when he had. "But judging by the position of the foal, it's still going to be a few hours."

He lifted an eyebrow.

Not sure whether he considered that good news or bad, she set down her vet bag. "In the meantime, we have a few things to do."

He let out a rough exhalation of breath. "Like...?"

"Sterilize and put fresh hay, water and feed in a nearby stall, so we can move them after the foal is born. We don't want to expose the foal to contamination."

"On it," Noah said. "In fact, I'll set up two stalls, just in case we need 'em."

Anything, Tess thought, *to keep him busy, and calm*. Short of sending him out to boil water, anyway.

She handed him a pair of veterinary coveralls, and a box of sterile birthing gloves. Then told him to put the coveralls on, and wait on the shoulder-length gloves until the time came when she did need his veterinary assistance.

"Were you there to witness the births of your girls?" she asked eventually.

Noah set up bales of hay against the stable walls, to act as seats for them. "Yes."

The muscles in his shoulders flexed as he worked. Aware this was a new side of him, Tess took in his handsome profile and smiled. "Were you nervous?"

He chuckled. "Yeah. Especially the first time." He shook his head ruefully, remembering. "I drove Shelby all the way to the hospital, then realized I left her suitcase in the front hall. I had to call a friend of ours to go by the house and get it. But that was the only snafu in labor and delivery. Lucy came out, feisty as ever."

Tess could imagine. She studied the tenderness etched on his face. "What about with the twins?"

His brows drew together. "It was a little easier, since I had been through the whole birth process once. But it was more stressful, in another sense, because we knew Shelby was having twins. And we didn't know how that would go."

"But it went fine," Tess guessed.

"Yep." He nodded, smiling. "Although it was a whole lot faster. It required twelve hours of labor for Lucy to come into the world. The twins were both here two hours after Shelby's water broke, so…we barely made it to the hospital."

Tess imagined what that must have been like. "Sounds exciting."

Noah smiled. "It was. To the point…" he went on, then suddenly stopped.

"What were you going to say?" Whatever it was, Tess noticed, it seemed to have surprised him.

He shrugged and turned to her. Serious, happy now. "That I wouldn't mind doing it all again."

Knowing Noah was open to having another child, was spirit lifting to say the least. Watching him worry over Miss Coco, as her labor progressed, was a lot more difficult.

"I've never heard her sound like that," Noah said an hour and a half later as the donkey brayed in pain. She had been pacing, but now she was lying back down again, on her side, her tail held back away from her body.

"That's because her baby is coming…" Birthing gloves on, Tess kneeled next to Miss Coco. She could see the tip of one sac-covered hoof, then part of one leg, coming through the opening. And…*oh, no!*

"What is it?" Noah asked in alarm, reading her expression.

"Both feet need to come out before the head, in what's called diving position. Right now, we've only got one. Get on the other side of her and keep her calm while I…" Tess gently nudged the baby donkey's nose back inside the mama, then reached around until she found the other front leg, and brought it out, too.

Her sides heaving with the force of her contractions, Miss Coco brayed all the louder. And then the foal's head began to emerge. Tess guided it out.

The rest of the foal's body followed swiftly. It was covered in a bluish gray membrane, filled with fluid. Tess broke the sack, pulling placental membranes off the newborn donkey's nostrils and muzzle. She checked for obstruction, relieved to find nothing that would hamper breathing, and rubbed the chest wall to encourage better air intake. As she peeled away the rest of the neonatal sack, she noted in relief that all was as it should be. "Confirmation is perfect," she told Noah happily. The thick-coated twenty-pound foal was the same cocoa color as her mother, with a white streak down the middle of her face, and white socks on all four legs.

Noah's broad shoulders sagged in relief. "That's great." He gazed down tenderly at the newly born animal. "How can I help?" he asked.

"Get her used to the sound of your voice, and your touch." Her heart filled to bursting by the miracle of birth, she nodded at the stack of clean, soft towels. "And use those to gently wipe her down."

Grinning, Noah kneeled beside Tess, who was tending to Miss Coco, and cared for the newborn donkey. "The girls are going to be thrilled to find out we have another female on the Welcome Ranch."

Tess caught the placenta and put it into a plastic basin, for later examination. "Definitely seems to be the trend," she said wryly. "You and Tank are outnumbered."

Noah chuckled.

Miss Coco lumbered to her feet, the action breaking the umbilical cord. While Noah doused the stump with a syringe of chlorhexidine solution, Tess cleaned Miss Coco's hindquarters and mammary glands with mild soap and water. Finished, they moved both animals to the already prepared stall across the aisleway.

An exhausted Miss Coco collapsed on the soft clean hay. They settled her baby next to her, within reach of a teat. Blinking in confusion, the baby turned away.

"Is that supposed to happen?" Noah asked.

"Not to worry. We can help her get the hang of nursing." While Noah continued imprinting the newborn with his soothing touch and low, encouraging voice, Tess grabbed what she needed from her bag of supplies. "First, we have to milk out two to four ounces and give her some colostrum from a bottle. The latter of which I'll let you do…"

Minutes later, Noah was sitting next to the mama's head, with his back against the stall wall, feeding the baby donkey with the expertise of a natural cowboy and veteran dad. Miss Coco looked on with a mix of contentment and fatigue. When the baby'd had her fill, they put the new jennet in the curve of her mama's body, to help them bond and keep the baby donkey warm. The two snuggled happily.

Tess tilted her head in the direction of the video camera Noah had mounted above the stall, to capture it all. "Your girls are going to love this."

Noah grinned, agreeing. "It'll be some home movie. Once we edit out all the goop, of course."

"And the scary sounds."

"Yep."

While Noah cleaned and disinfected the birth stall, Tess gathered up all her vet gear.

She and Noah both stripped off their shoulder-length gloves and coveralls, put them into a large trash bag for later disposal and faced off in the aisleway. Aware they made a pretty good team, even in as potentially stressful a situation as this, she pushed aside the sudden fierce desire to bring him all the way into her arms and kiss him passionately.

"So now what?" he asked softly, looking handsome and strong in his dark plaid flannel shirt and jeans. Like he wanted to kiss her, too.

Aware how hard it would be to stop, once they opened the door to something like that, she drew a bracing breath. Focused on what still lay ahead. "We wait to make sure the foal is strong enough to stand and nurse."

"Then we might as well get comfortable," Noah said. He got another six-foot-wide bale of hay and set it in the corner of the big roomy horse stall, where the donkeys were now quartered. Then left again briefly, returning with two cold electrolyte drinks. Their fingers brushed, then their bodies as they settled on the bale, their backs to the wall in the heated stable.

"Thanks," Tess said.

Noah nudged her arm, snuggling comfortably

against her, too. "So tell me, Doc," he murmured softly. "What was it like, the first time you did this…?"

For the next hour or so, Noah and Tess traded animal husbandry stories—Tess's warm, womanly presence and soft voice was like a balm to his soul.

He talked about things he had seen on the Circle L. Albeit he'd been more of a watcher from a distance than a hands-on guy, until tonight. She told him about some of her most challenging cases. "Although I think this might be my most joyful," she said.

An hour after that, the newborn stood on wobbly legs and nosed her mama. With a muted groan, Miss Coco stood, and the baby attempted—unsuccessfully—to latch on to a teat. Only to fall onto the soft hay.

Noah leaned forward to jump to the rescue. But Tess held him back. "Let them try to work it out first."

Miss Coco licked her newborn gently. The baby donkey stood again, wobbling mightily as she headed for a teat. This time Miss Coco adjusted toward her body, too.

Only to have the foal fail and fall again.

Noah groaned. "This is torture," he said.

Tess remained confident. "They'll get it."

And sure enough, the next time they did. The little one latched on and began to nurse. The thirsty, suckling sounds filled the stable. And for long moments, all Noah and Tess could do was hold on to each other and take in the beauty and wonder of it all.

* * *

Around midnight, Noah went back to the house and returned with a big thermos of coffee and sandwiches for the two of them. Miss Coco and her baby had both lied down to rest, with the little one curled up against her mama's chest. The snuggling was greeting-card cute. Tess couldn't stop smiling, watching them.

He couldn't stop smiling, either, watching *her*. He nudged her thigh with his bent knee. "Is this the reason why you became a vet?"

She finished her sandwich and put the wadded-up wrapper back in the insulated bag. "One of them."

He leaned in close enough to track the luscious softness of her lips. "But I'm guessing this is one of your favorite parts?"

For a moment, he thought she wouldn't answer, then she shrugged, a flash of hurt in her expression. "Recently, I've come to accept that bringing animals into the world is the closest I will ever come to being a mom."

He paused, not sure what she was trying to tell him. Was there a health issue? Did she think that would affect how he saw her...?

Reading his mind, she lifted a hand. "There's no physical reason why not. Not that I know of, anyway. But..." She breathed in deeply, frowning. "I know how hard it was for my mom to bring me up on her own, how lonely it was for me. And maybe it's selfish. Or foolish. But I don't think I ever want to go that route." She raked her teeth across her lower lip.

"If I had a family, it would have to be because I was married, and it was what my husband wanted, too."

He caught her hand in his. "I get it. And you're right. It's damn hard to parent on your own, even with a zillion family members nearby, ready and willing to help. Not to mention, offer advice."

Recalling the romantic coaching he had recently received from his sister Jillian, he winced.

Tess grinned, as always, sharing his sense of humor. "I hadn't thought about it that way." She clasped his hand tightly in return. "Maybe being an only child had its perks, too."

He loved the way her eyes lit up when she smiled. "You never had to fight over the last cookie," he pointed out.

"Or wait forever for my turn in the bathroom. Still—" she released her palm from his and went back to sipping her coffee "—being an only kid was lonely so I think if I ever were to embark on motherhood, I'd definitely want to have at least three or four kids."

And I've always wanted a son. Plus, I have three daughters who would really like to have a mother again, and possibly another sibling, too.

Not that if he had another baby, it would have to be a boy. A girl would be great, too. He turned to Tess, easily imagining how beautiful she would be with child. *His* child.

Was it too much, too soon, to even be thinking about? Noah couldn't say. All he knew for sure was that sitting there next to her, in the quiet of the stable, he was finally ready to put the loss of Shelby behind him. Move on to a fuller life. As well as tempted to volunteer to help Tess achieve her dreams. To give her reason for staying on at the Welcome Ranch with them, and becoming more and more a part of their lives.

Chapter Twelve

Tess and Noah spent the night in the stable, keeping watch over mama and baby donkey. They talked about everything and nothing, exactly as they would have had they been on a date. Or two. Or three. And even as the hours passed, they never ran out of anything to say.

Shortly after dawn, the baby donkey finished nursing again. Satisfied both mama and baby were doing well, and no longer needed constant monitoring, Tess went back to the house to shower and get some sleep. Noah set out feed and water for Miss Coco, then mucked out the stall and headed back to the house, too.

The house was so quiet he figured she was already asleep. A little disappointed their intimate time together had come to an end, he headed for the shower, too. While he was getting dressed, the scent of something delicious filled the air.

Curious, he went downstairs. Tess was in the kitchen, looking gorgeous as could be in a soft flannel shirt, jeans and shearling lined ankle boots. Her curly hair was damp and swept into an unruly mass on the back of her head. She wasn't wearing any makeup. But she didn't need any.

He peered over her shoulder, drinking in the scent of her citrus perfume. "Either you made enough for two or you're hungry as a lumberjack," he murmured, as if her cooking for him like this was no big deal, when in fact it was a *very* big deal.

Her smile bloomed. "Ha ha, cowboy. Of course, I cooked for you, too."

He moved in, eying the sheet pan full of golden-brown toast, topped with thin slices of ham, mounds of grated gruyere cheese and béchamel sauce. "Croque madame?" he guessed, recalling her mother's expertise in French cuisine.

She topped each sandwich with another piece of toast, added more ham, gruyere and béchamel, then slid the sheet pan into the oven, to broil.

"Mmm-hmm." She swirled butter into the skillet on the stove, and added eggs with the skill of an experienced cook. "It's the perfect dish to eat any time of day."

He let his glance drift over her admiringly. Hands braced on her hips, he brought her against him. "Anything you cook would be perfect to eat any time of day."

Tess splayed her palms across his chest, and tipped her face up to his. She sighed contentedly, looking as happy and relaxed as he felt. "Flattery will get you a post doing dishes."

"Gratefully, darlin'." He tipped an imaginary hat at her. As ready to eat what she had prepared for them, as he was to make love with her again.

Tess nodded at the lightly dressed greens in a bowl. "Want to carry that to the table for me?"

Noah nodded, touched by all she had done. "Love to." *Love you*…he almost said.

An unexpected silence hung out between them. Tess wasn't sure what was wrong. She only knew that something in Noah came to a full stop. With a shake of his head, as if that would clear it, he turned away. Deep in thought, he finished setting the table.

Telling herself it was nothing—that he was probably just as tired as she was, after their very long night—she finished off the entrée and brought the plates over, too.

"Damn, this is good," he said after taking the first bite.

She returned his grin. "Thanks."

His gaze turned tender. "Thank you for doing this for us."

A thrill swept through Tess. Was that more than gratitude in his eyes? Or was she just hoping to see what she wanted to see there? Affection? Connection? The possibility of more? All she knew for certain was that she secretly wanted all of those things from him. And more.

That did not mean, however, they were on the same page.

With effort, she pushed aside her romantic musings, and went back to the conversation, and the fact he was surprised she had gone to so much trouble for him. When the truth was, she was stunned to realize how much she had wanted to cook just for him, too. Because it was the kind of thing a wife did? Or because it would deepen the man-woman intimacy between them? Which it already had.

Noticing how quiet it was without the kids, she said, "I kind of owed you after the way you helped me in the stable all last night."

The camaraderie between them deepening all the more, he toasted orange-juice glasses with her. "They're our family donkeys."

She sipped her juice. "Still…a lot of guys would have left it to the vet."

He shook his head, his deep blue eyes still locked with hers. "Not me," he told her huskily. "I wanted to stay."

A surge of awareness flowed through her. She realized just how close she was to falling all the way in love with him. "I'm glad you did."

They were quiet for a while after that. But it was the good kind of silence. The type that came when two people were so comfortable with each other that they didn't feel the need to fill up every moment with endless polite chatter.

Finished, Noah sat back in his chair. Tess leaned back in hers, too. He looked around, as if trying to figure out what he could do for her now. "Coffee?" he asked finally.

His low, husky voice sent curls of longing through her midriff. She knew she should get up and start the dishes, but she was too comfy right where she was, and she did not want this moment between them to end with something as mundane as daily chores. "No. I've still got too much adrenaline as it is."

"Yeah." He stretched out his long legs, his knee nudging hers beneath the table. "I know what you mean." He shifted again. They were no longer touching. "I feel like I should be sleeping…"

"But you can't. Not yet."

"Right."

They fell silent once again.

She gazed around.

He reached across the table and covered her hand with his. "What are you thinking?"

How much I adore your touch. Your kiss. Your… everything.

Aware she might be pushing the envelope, since all they had agreed upon up to now was a secret no-strings fling—making love only on the previous two Wednesdays, when the kids were at school and she had the morning off… Yes, they had spent time together off and on, but there had been no mention of taking it further. Only taking it slow, and letting the situation evolve day by day.

Aware he was still waiting for her to explain what she'd been thinking, she pushed aside her forbidden feelings, and cleared her throat, and talked about the other thing on her mind. The thing that struck her every time she stepped in his house. "About how much I love your home. It's so cozy and warm and welcoming." She gestured at the big, modern living area, with the floor-to-ceiling windows. The modern fireplace, and even more state-of-the-art kitchen. Even his work area, with the big L-shaped desk and all the computer monitors, was somehow comforting. Maybe because it seemed to signify that even when he was working, he was always still right there, for whatever his girls, his pets, even her...needed.

He took her other hand in his, too. Clasping both warmly, he made a funny face at her. "Well, it is the Welcome Ranch."

She rolled her eyes. She could so get used to his bad jokes. His easy ability to make her smile. Just like she could so get used to staying here, with him, and his kids...

She frowned. He noticed.

"And that's a problem because...?" He let go of her and sat back.

Tess gestured vaguely. "I'm not sure if mine will ever be that way, even after all the work is done." She forced herself to stand, before she gave away even more of her private insecurities. "A few throws and the right pillows can only do so much..."

She knew animals.

She did *not* know families, or how to navigate them. Never mind one as complex as Noah's...

He joined her at the sink as they started to do their dishes. She scraped and rinsed. He loaded them into the dishwasher.

Once again, they were working like two halves of a whole—his strong, masculine presence a balm to her troubled soul.

His shoulder nudged hers, sending a frisson of warmth down her arm. "First of all, I have faith your home will be a lot like you," he told her in the kind, comforting tone she loved. "Which means it will be wonderful, inviting, the kind of place where people are going to want to come and hang out with you."

Listening intently, she gazed over at him. Happy to have someone to talk to who was so understanding.

"Second, once your home is done, and you move out of here, it's not going to be like you are locked in there, alone." He shut the dishwasher door with his knee. As they turned to face each other, they dried their hands on the same towel.

He made an inclusive gesture. "You can invite people like me and the kids over, or sometimes just me." His lips curved in amorous invitation. "And you can come here any time you want as well. To be with us."

He caught her wrists and reeled her in, not stopping until she was flush against him. "Because in case you haven't noticed—" he slid a hand down her spine and back up again "—there is a guest room with your name on it." He paused to tuck a strand of hair behind her ear. "And we love having you here, so you will always be welcome here," he told her gruffly.

She smiled despite herself. "You really mean that, don't you?"

His eyes glinted happily. "With all my heart, yeah, I do, darlin'."

The next thing Tess knew, his mouth was lowering toward hers. Their lips met in an explosion of heat and need. One kiss turned into another, and then another. And they were headed upstairs, bypassing her bedroom for his.

Noah knew he wasn't playing fair. Using this time alone to show her how much their attraction for each other could change things. For both of them. If they would both open their minds and hearts up to the possibilities, that was.

He shut the door behind them and, his lips still fused to hers, trapped her against the wall. Gasping, she laughed in surprise as he kissed his way from her cheek, to the lobe of her ear, to the open vee of her button-up flannel.

She gasped again, trembling now. "Noah…"

He drew back, to look into her eyes. Wanting to make sure she was fully on board. "I want you in my bed."

"Then what are you waiting for…?" She took his head in her hands, sifting her hands through his hair, and slowly, effortlessly brought their mouths back together.

His body roared to life.

Lower still, where she surged against him, trembling with need, he felt the soft, sweet bliss of her surrender. The first contact of their lips sent another jolt to his system. The way she was pressing against him let him know that she was already as turned on as he was.

Excitement coursing through him, he unbuttoned her shirt and undid the front clasp of her bra. Her breasts came tumbling out, and he caught them with his hands, rubbing the soft globes and taut nipples with the flat of his palms.

She moaned in response. "Two can play at this game, cowboy," she purred. Her hands gripped the bottom of his sweater and she pulled it up over his head. His T-shirt went the same way. Then her shirt and bra.

Naked from the waist up, he brought her closer still, so they were skin-to-skin. The unyielding surface of the wall still behind them.

"You are so sexy," she murmured, running her hands across his shoulders, down his back.

The caution that had been in her eyes from the start was not there now. "You think so?"

"Mmm..."

That was all the encouragement it took. He covered her jutting nipples with his hands, felt them press into his palms as he lowered his mouth to hers. This time, she was more than ready for him, her lips opening to the pressure of his. She went up on tiptoe, arching wantonly, giving even as she took. Causing him to shudder in response.

Needing more, he dropped his hands and wrapped his arms around her, fusing her with heat. She let out a soft, acquiescent sigh, at the friction of her bare breasts rubbing against his chest.

Impatient, she found the buckle on his belt.

He found hers.

Laughing, they kept going until they were both free of any impediment. Her delicate hands found and claimed him. He throbbed beneath her tender touch.

"Tess…"

He caught her to him and, still kissing her, danced her backward to the bed. Then he swept back the covers with one hand, and they tumbled down onto the sheets. He lay beside her, making his own demands now, stroking the insides of her thighs, the rounded curves of her buttocks and the sweet femininity of her lower abdomen. She whimpered as he slid his hand over her mound, tracing the flowering petals, exploring inside and out. Again and then again. Until they were both on the precipice of making this fantasy come true.

He found the protection they needed. She strained against him. He lifted her hips, and then they were one.

She was climaxing, opening herself up, inviting him deeper, deeper still. Until there was no more waiting, only feeling, only wanting her to be his. That swiftly, he followed her over the edge.

* * *

Tess caught her breath and collapsed against Noah's chest, her body still throbbing with the force of her orgasm. She felt sated behind her most erotic dreams and yet she already wanted him again. How wild was that?

No more outrageous than the notion that they might be on the verge of falling in love with each other.

Except…she couldn't let herself think like that.

Noah had already been married. Had a wife. And now three kids and a very busy life.

Right now, it was easy to see each other, because she was living with him.

Soon, it wouldn't be.

At least not the way it was now…she thought with a frown, trying not to sigh.

"I've got three requests," Noah murmured, stroking a hand through her hair.

"Three!" Tess echoed, peering at him from beneath her lashes. Tamping down the yearning welling inside her heart, she returned his coaxing grin with a playful smile of her own. "That's *a lot*."

He chuckled, as if to say, guilty as charged. "Mmm-hmm. My first ask is we stop pretending that we don't have something pretty special going on here."

She drew back to look at him, not ready to agree to anything until she knew the rest of what he wanted from her. She splayed her hands across his chest, her body still aching for more. More kisses. More lovemaking. More unbelievable pleasure. "And the second?"

"I want us to spend this evening and all of tomorrow morning together, since the kids aren't here. And we don't have to worry about them seeing us in a compromising position. Third, I want you in my bed with me all night long."

She pursed her lips. "Those are some pretty big asks, cowboy."

"To match what we've got going on."

He was right. This would either bring them closer, or show them they weren't right for anything more than a fling, after all.

"Okay," she returned softly, then decided to make one more stipulation. "I'll do everything you ask, providing if whatever this is between us doesn't work out the way we both think it might, that we find a way to take a step back and be friends."

For a moment, she thought he might argue with her, insist they were meant for more, so a fall-back plan would not be necessary. But then he relaxed. "Friends forever, I promise."

"Me, too." Tess slid back into his arms, aware he was as ready to make love again as she was. She didn't know what the future held, only the present. And for now, she thought as they came together with hot, burning passion, the present was enough.

The next twenty-four hours passed blissfully. With them treasuring every second alone together. Just before noon, Noah received a call from his mom. "They're about ten minutes away." He grabbed his jacket, then handed her hers. "I suggested they meet us at the stable." Tank followed them out the door.

Tess fell into step behind him. The morning was sunny and clear and cold. All in all, a beautiful winter day. Struggling to go back to a more casual reality after a romantic weekend alone, she asked, "Do your folks know about the baby donkey's birth?"

"Yeah, I texted them Friday night. Asked them not to say anything because we wanted it to be a surprise for the girls."

"Speaking of things not to be shared..." She tucked her hand in his. "What happened..." she began nervously.

Noah gave her a solemn smile, guessing where she was going with this. "Is just between the two of us."

She released a relieved breath. She didn't want to risk anything happening to wreck the intimacy they'd found. Too much outside scrutiny, too soon, just might. "Yes."

Noah looked at her gently. "Don't worry. I don't want to share this with anyone, either."

He opened up the stable door, ducked inside with her and paused to kiss her sweetly. Outside, Tank gave a little woof. They heard the sound of his parents' SUV. They quickly drew apart and headed back outside, in plain view, standing a casual distance apart.

As soon as the car was parked, the girls came tumbling out. "We're home!" Lucy, Avery and Angelica shouted in unison. They raced to greet both Tess and

Noah, hugging them both. Tess hugged the girls back, enjoying their exuberance.

The kids continued all talking at once. "We went to the zoo!" Avery declared.

"And the science museum!" Lucy put in.

"And had *two* sleepovers, too!" Angelica said.

Noah beamed. "Sounds like you had a great time. What do you say to your grandparents?"

A round of happy thank-yous followed.

"We'll leave their things in the house, and then get going," Robert said.

Noah looked at his dad. "You don't want to stay?"

His mom smiled, speaking in code. "We know you have a lot to do, and we do, too. So we'll visit later in the week."

More hugs followed. Carol and Robert drove off.

The girls looked at him and Tess, suddenly realizing something different was going on here, although they hadn't figured out what yet.

"We have a special surprise for you," Noah said.

Lucy gasped. Her initial scowl at having been left out turned to an expression of delight. "Miss Coco had her baby?"

"She did," Noah confirmed. He held out his hand to Lucy, giving Tess a look that asked her to do the same, so she took charge of the twins. "And Tess and I are going to take you into the stable to see them."

Chapter Thirteen

Noah paused just inside the stable doors, to make eye contact with each of his three daughters. "Remember, girls, we don't want to upset Miss Coco or scare the baby donkey, so we have to be super quiet and careful. Okay?"

All three of them nodded.

As discussed, they went into the stall with Tess, one at a time, and petted first Coco, then her little one, gently and tenderly. When they had finished, and stepped back into the aisleway to observe a little longer, the little one stood and began to nurse.

"Oh, Daddy, the baby is so pretty," Lucy whispered, already completely in love with their newest pet.

"And fluffy," Avery admired wonderingly.

"And the same color as her mama," Angelica gushed.

Lucy turned to Tess. Her brow furrowed. "I forgot to ask. Is it a boy or girl donkey?"

"It's a female."

"What's her name?" the eight-year-old asked.

"We were waiting for you to help with that," Noah said.

Less patiently, Lucy demanded, "Well, what have you been calling her?"

"Baby..." Noah replied, very softly. He put his index finger against his lips, reminding them to keep their voices low and soothing, too.

Lucy broke out in a triumphant grin, before dropping her voice back to a stage whisper. "Then that's what we should name her!"

"Yes! *Baby!*" the twins echoed gleefully, whispering, too.

For a moment, Noah looked gobsmacked. Tess thought the idea was as cute as the three little girls. Finally, he rubbed his hand across his jaw and drawled, "Well, we can talk about it a little more—"

"Nope," Lucy interrupted importantly. She sent her sisters a bolstering glance. "*Baby* is what we want to call her."

Her sisters nodded in agreement.

Seeming to realize, as Tess did in that moment, just how rarely the girls came to terms on anything, right out of the gate, Noah exchanged a glance with her, then gave in. "It's settled then. Her name is Baby."

Lucy started to clap, then remembering the need

to be quiet while the foal nursed, put her hands on her hips instead.

For a while, they all watched the wonder of mother and baby, and the free-flowing love between them. The miracle of life never failed to astound Tess.

She was pleased to see the girls and Noah were similarly affected.

Finally, Baby walked a short distance away and lied down on the hay. Miss Coco stretched out next to her. Both looked ready for a nap.

Noah motioned for his daughters to follow him.

They tiptoed out and Tess took up the rear. As they left the stable, Lucy piped up in her normal voice. "Daddy, did you make a movie of Baby being born?"

He smiled and wrapped an arm around her shoulders. "We did. Tess helped me edit it."

The twins fell in step on either side of Tess, reaching for her hands, as if she was their mother. A wave of sentiment rushed through her. Realizing how much she was going to miss moments like this, if things didn't work out between her and Noah, she took hold of their palms, fighting back the unprecedented ache in her throat.

Lucy pulled Noah toward the house. "Can we see the movie now?" Angelica asked.

He turned to give Tess and the twins a sweeping glance. She thought she saw a gleam of approval in his eyes. "Sure!" he said.

He already had the TV all set up and settled the girls on the sofa with him and Tess. The film was short and sweet, with everything potentially too much for three-year-olds to witness cut out.

The twins curiosity faded as quickly as it had appeared. Avery slipped off the sofa. "Daddy, can we go see our doll babies upstairs?"

"Yeah, we want to play with them," Angelica added.

"That sounds like a great idea," he said.

Able to see as well as Tess that a storm was coming on, he went to get the computer tablet they had already set up, just for the eight-year-old.

"That wasn't a very good movie, Daddy," Lucy complained, leaping to her feet.

Tess felt a meltdown coming on.

Accepting his daughter's disappointed criticism with a nod, Noah sat on the sofa, leaving a cozy space between him and Tess. He patted the empty cushion between them. "It was perfect for the twins, Lucy. But you're right, you do need something geared for an eight-year-old." He beckoned her with a kind, loving glance that melted Tess's heart.

"So come and sit with us on the sofa, and we will show you the more grown-up version on the computer tablet, that Tess and I worked on, just for you."

The home movie was still cut to avoid anything too gross or scary. But it did show Baby coming out in full diving position, blinking and looking around for the first time, then being dried off with a towel. The footage also included Noah feeding her colostrum from a baby bottle, and Baby's faltering first attempts to stand and then nurse. Relaxing music, suitable for a kid's nature movie, filled the background on this version, too.

As Tess had expected, Lucy had a lot of questions. Tess answered them one by one.

When she had finished, his daughter wrapped her arms fiercely around Tess and said, "Thank you for taking care of Miss Coco and Baby and helping Daddy make the movie for me."

Her heart filling with gratitude—that Noah and his beautiful children had come into her life—Tess fought the emotion rising in her throat. The sudden impulse to burst into tears. A wave of fierce maternal love sifting through her, Tess hugged Lucy back.

"I was happy to do it," she murmured thickly. She leaned back so she could look into the vulnerable little girl's eyes. "And just so you know, our work with Miss Coco and Baby is just beginning. They are going to need a lot of care. You can help with that—as long as there is a grown-up nearby."

Lucy looked at Noah for confirmation.

"I'm fully on board with that," he said, giving Tess a grateful look.

Was this what it would feel like to co-parent with him? To step into the mother's role in this adorable family?

Tess only knew she liked the feeling, very much.

"I don't know what's wrong with her," Noah murmured to Tess several hours later.

Lucy was outside by herself, desolately sitting on

a swing, rhythmically kicking the ground beneath her feet. Upset that she couldn't play with Baby, for hours on end, the way she had played with Tank when he was a puppy? And instead was relegated to just visiting twice a day? She had gone into a funk she showed no signs of relinquishing.

Tess joined him at the window. Their arms brushed briefly. As always, she had endless patience for his emotionally volatile eldest daughter. She moved closer and gave him a soothing smile. "I think she is just overtired."

He remained where he was, the warmth of her body transmitting to his. Then swiveled slightly, making no effort to hide his worry. "Then why won't she consent to taking a nap like her little sisters?" Who had fallen asleep, shortly after they had gotten home, on the upstairs playroom floor. And were napping still.

Tess gave him an appreciative grin, letting him know in that instant just how much she had learned about his kids since living at the ranch. "Because she's eight. And third graders don't take naps on purpose."

He exhaled. "I still feel like there is something else bugging her." Something he needed to further investigate. If his daughter would ever let him.

Tess touched his forearm gently. Her voice was as commiserating as her gaze. "Well, here is your chance, cowboy. She's stomping our way."

The back door opened and shut, more loudly than

needed. Lucy took off her jacket and dropped it on the mudroom floor. Noah lifted his eyebrows. The child sighed, picked it up and put it on the hook, then came all the way into the kitchen. She slapped her hands on her hips, frustration bubbling up. "Daddy, I'm bored!"

"Well, you could read a book," Noah offered calmly. "Or watch one of your favorite programs on TV."

Lucy vetoed both with a shake of her head.

Suddenly, he had the sudden sense this was all working up to something. "Is there something you'd like to do?" he asked mildly.

"Well..." Lucy tensed nervously, then sent a hopeful look Tess's way. She inhaled deeply. "Maybe Tess could teach me to bake something."

The last thing he wanted to do was put Tess on the spot. He was about to interject when Tess lifted a staying palm, and smiled at Lucy so warmly his moody daughter smiled back in return.

"Baking sounds fun." Tess sat down at the kitchen island and gestured for the youngster to join her. "In fact, that is one of the things I like to do to relax. What would you like to learn to make?"

Lucy slid onto the stool next to Tess, then announced decisively, "*Not* scones. You taught all my aunts to make those."

Tess tilted her head, giving admirable weight to his eldest daughter's need to feel special. "Good point."

Encouraged, Lucy continued, "Maybe something I could put in my lunchbox and take to school. But it can't be cookies or brownies or cake. My teacher said we have to eat healthy at lunchtime."

Tess absorbed that statement with the importance in which it had been delivered. "Is banana bread okay?"

Lucy's smile faded. "That's what Bethany takes to school. She makes it with her mom. But I don't like banana bread."

Was this where this was coming from? She was in competition from a classmate? Or maybe just feeling left out because she no longer had a mom? Noah's heart went out to her.

Judging from the kind way Tess was looking at Lucy, she was feeling the same way he was. Like all she wanted to do was ease his little girl's pain. Make her life as carefree as a kid's life should be.

Tess's eyes lit up. Her cheeks took on a gorgeous pink. "I might have an idea." She whipped out her cell phone. "Have you ever had apple-fritter bread?"

Lucy shook her head.

Noah had no idea what it was, either.

Tess typed something into her phone. She pulled up a recipe with a photo. "Feel up to trying this? It's got chunks of apple and applesauce, and cinnamon in it. And a light apple glaze on top."

Lucy lit up, the way she used to when Shelby included her in the kitchen. "That looks yummy," she said sincerely.

Tess returned her enthusiasm. "Then we'll try it!"

"I used to bake stuff with my mom," Lucy told

Tess, as they got the dry ingredients out of the pantry and set them on the kitchen island.

"Me, too." Tess's smile was a little sad. She gently touched Lucy's shoulder, then helped his daughter put on an apron. "You must miss doing that."

"I do." Lucy turned back to Tess, looking like she wanted to give her another hug, but was a little too shy to try. "But sometimes my grandma lets me cook with her at the Circle L. It's fun. But…" She sighed. "It's not really the same as being with my mom and making stuff."

Tess tied an apron on, too, looking so at home in his kitchen Noah wasn't sure how he was going to feel when she eventually left.

Maybe Lucy wasn't the only one in trouble…

"I get that," Tess returned candidly. "My mom died almost ten years ago, and I still miss her. But I have a lot of good memories and I try to concentrate on those, and hold them here," she said, placing a hand over her heart.

Lucy nodded seriously. "That's what I do, too."

Which meant, Noah mused in relief, Lucy had retained a lot of what she had learned in her grief-support group for kids, back in California.

Noah brewed a cup of coffee while they went to the fridge, and got out those ingredients, too.

"How come you don't have kids?" Lucy blurted.

So much for things going smoothly, Noah thought with a wince. "Lucy!" he interjected. "You know better than to ask a grown-up something personal like that."

Tess turned to Noah. "I don't mind."

He could see she didn't. Another plus in her favor.

She focused on Lucy. "The reason I don't have kids of my own is because I haven't been lucky enough to have any."

Tess's answer came easily.

Which meant she had thought about it.

At least in the last few weeks.

"But do you want some?" Lucy asked.

Did she? Not too long ago, when she had first arrived in Laramie, and been so standoffish initially, and careful not to intrude in his family life, Noah would have said probably not. Even though she was very good with kids.

Tess paused thoughtfully, this time not looking at Noah at all. "I'm beginning to think I might want to be a mom someday, after all," she said softly.

At eight that evening, Tess had just picked up the remote and settled on the sofa, when Noah came into the living room. Flashing her a lazy grin and sporting a day's worth of stubble, he was the picture of rugged masculinity. As he sat down beside her, she felt her heart give a little jolt. Why did he have to be so darn attractive? And why couldn't she stop wanting to be naked with him again, even though she knew that kind of intimacy made her emotionally vulnerable.

His gaze drifted over her, taking in her flannel-lined jeans and red wool sweater. His voice dropped to a tantalizing rumble. "You made Lucy's week, cooking with her this afternoon."

She stopped scrolling through the channels long enough to spare him a flirtatious glance. "You saw us slicing up and wrapping the individual pieces of apple-fritter bread for her lunches?"

"Yep," he said in open admiration. "Luckily there was some left for everyone to have with dinner." He covered her hand with his. "Anyway, thank you for doing that."

She loved the fact he took anything related to his kids' happiness so seriously. Aware this was the kind of thing they would be doing if they were married— hanging out together after the kids were in bed— she confessed, "It was good for me, too, you know."

As she turned to him, she inadvertently brushed up against him even more. Their hips were touching. He didn't move away, and neither did she. "I haven't done anything mother-daughter like that for a very long time. Not that she and I are mother and daughter," Tess corrected awkwardly, catching a whiff of his masculine scent. "But…"

He chuckled at her self-conscious manner. "I know what you mean."

They exchanged glances.

He squinted at her affectionately. "Lucy's not the only one who was a little spoiled with attention this weekend, though."

She tried not to think how intimate it felt, sitting here together, with the evening stretching endlessly out ahead of them.

Pretending not to know whom he was really referring to, she said playfully, "Miss Coco?"

He wrapped his arm around her and tucked her into the curve of his body. "Me." He pressed a kiss on the top of her head, then his dark eyebrows knit in frustration. "I don't know how I'm going to get by not having any alone time with you."

Tess pursed her lips. Their eyes met and held. "Well, I am usually off Wednesday mornings," she reminded him.

He rubbed the inside of her wrist with the pad of his thumb. And regarded her in a way that left no doubt they would be making love again very soon. "Brunch here after the kids are in school?"

She loved the romantic turn their conversation was taking. The fact he was trying to nail down the next time they were together, instead of just letting things happen at will. She splayed her hand across the hardness of his denim-covered thigh. A melting sensation started deep inside her. "Brunch sounds nice."

"To me, too." He flashed her a warm smile, similar to the one he gave her when he was about to ravish her. "But what really sounds good is an actual date." He put his hand over hers, trapping it against his muscular thigh. "Will you let me take you out?"

Telling herself this was not the time or place to indulge in her most tantalizing fantasies, not when his three kids were sleeping right upstairs, she re plied in her most matter-of-fact tone, "Yes. But not until I move into my own place."

He leaned closer and brushed his lips against hers. "And when will that be?"

"My furniture is supposed to be delivered somewhere between the thirteenth of February and the sixteenth. I'll know more as the time gets closer. Kind of depends on what else is on the moving truck, and where it has to be delivered."

"Gotcha. So—" eyes crinkling at the corners, he paused to calculate "—you'll still be here for around twelve more days?" He seemed as pleased about that as she was.

She turned, gliding her hands across the sinewy warmth of his chest. "Mmm-hmm. I'm not sure whether to wish for the thirteenth for delivery, though," she added wryly.

He chuckled with undisguised affection. "Why not?"

Trying not to wonder if he was becoming as serious about her as she was about him, she said, "It's a Friday." She wrinkled her nose. "So maybe it'd be good if it wasn't delivered on February the thirteenth."

He shook his head, drawing her closer still. "Ha ha. I'm not superstitious."

"Good to know," Tess said, flirting back as he stroked a hand lovingly through her hair. "And all joking aside, neither am I."

She laid her head on his shoulder, sighing contentedly. He kissed her temple, the curve of her cheek, the shell of her ear. "Well, however it works out, *when-ever* it works out," he told her huskily, looking deep into her eyes, "I can't wait for our first date."

Chapter Fourteen

It felt like Tess had just gone to sleep, late Sunday evening, when she felt a light tap on her shoulder. She opened her eyes to find Lucy standing next to her bed, in the dark guest room.

Tess sat up against the pillows and turned on her bedside lamp. The bedroom was diffused with soft light.

Lucy's lower lip trembled. Panicked, she told Tess, "Something is wrong with Tank. He's crying and he won't get up."

That did *not* sound good. Wide-awake now, Tess tossed back the covers. "Where is he?"

"My room." Lucy took her hand and led her there.

Tank was curled up on the pink polka-dot dog cushion next to Lucy's bed. Tess could tell by the way the chocolate Lab was panting he was definitely in pain. She wondered if this was why he had been so quiet and lethargic all day, rarely venturing from the house even when everyone else went out to the stable.

She touched Lucy's shoulder gently. "Let me go get my vet bag. I'll be right back."

The child nodded, and sat down next to Tank, petting his back gently. "I'll stay here," she promised.

When Tess returned, she got out her stethoscope. Tank's heart rate was a little fast, given he was reclining, but his lungs were fine. She examined him, finding nothing amiss, until she went to touch his ears and he winced and let out a little whine of pain.

Tess got out her otoscope. His ears were definitely inflamed, with a funky smell and discharge inside the ear canal. "He's got an ear infection, honey." She got two swabs out of her bag, gently sampled the gunk in each ear and then slid each test into a plastic bag that she sealed for examination later.

Lucy watched, mesmerized. She continued petting Tank soothingly. Comforted, he curled into her touch. The young girl looked at Tess anxiously. "Can you give him some medicine or something?"

Tess nodded. "Absolutely." She got what she needed out of her vet bag and showed it all to Lucy. "But before we do that," she said as she twisted the application cap on the bottle, to open, "we're going to clean his ears with this solution." Tess held up his ear flap and squirted some in. She lowered the flap, and Tank immediately shook his head.

"He's trying to get it out!" Lucy protested.

Tess smiled reassuringly. "He's also spreading it

around inside the ear canal, and pushing out the gunk in there, along with the liquid cleaner I just put in. So that's a good thing." When he had settled, Tess wiped the inside of his ear with some cotton balls. Her heart went out to Tank as he winced and whimpered a little in pain.

Lucy teared up. "He's hurting," she said, her lower lip trembling again.

"Not to worry." Tess did his other ear, and then showed Lucy the tube of medicine she had pulled out of her bag. "This ointment I'm going to put in has a numbing agent as well as antibacterial and antifungal medicine. So he'll be better in no time."

Quickly, she applied seven drops of medicine to the inside of each ear. Finished, she rubbed the medication in by gently massaging his ear flaps. She urged Lucy to do the same.

Tank stopped whining and panting, and within another minute or two, completely relaxed.

Lucy smiled at her chocolate Lab then grinned up at Tess. "You did it! You made him all better."

"Yes," a low masculine voice murmured, breaking the middle-of-the-night silence, "she sure did."

They both turned to look.

Tess caught her breath. Noah was lounging in the open doorway, his hair rumpled, looking sexy as all get-out in a pair of pajama pants and a cotton T-shirt. It was clear he had been there for a while.

He strolled into the room. Then hunkered down next to Lucy and Tank. Hugging her, while petting their dog, he looked at his daughter soberly. "But you probably should have come to get me, instead of Tess, sweetheart."

Lucy turned back to Tess, immediately contrite. It was clear the thought hadn't even occurred to her. Which made sense since Tess was the animal doc, not Noah. The distressed expression was back on her young face. "I'm sorry I woke you up in the middle of the night," Lucy told her sincerely.

Knowing this was one thing the child did not need to worry about, Tess took her into her arms and embraced her tenderly. "Oh, honey, it's okay." She stroked her hair lightly, before letting her go and sitting back on her heels. "I'm glad I was here to take care of Tank. And even if I hadn't been here at the ranch, you could have called me, and I would have come out to see what was wrong."

"Really?" Lucy's face lit up with surprise and delight.

"Really," she said, meaning it with all her heart.

Noah sent her a questioning look she didn't quite understand. Then he turned back to his daughter, and reminded gently, "Tomorrow's a school day, Lucy. You need to go back to sleep."

Lucy made a face. "But I'm not sleepy now, Daddy."

Tank sat up on his cushion, looking concerned.

Like the family pet, Tess sensed an argument coming on.

In an effort to help Noah, she told Lucy, "I understand where you're coming from, honey. I feel pretty wide-awake now, too. But the thing is… Tank needs his sleep, so he can get better. And he will settle down faster, if he thinks you are going back to sleep, too."

"I'll bring you some warm milk," Noah offered.

Lucy lit up. "With vanilla and sugar like Mommy used to make?"

Noah hugged his daughter and helped her climb back into bed. "Exactly like she used to make," he promised.

Leaving them to talk privately, Tess eased out of the room. She was happy Shelby was still so much a part of their lives. That was a very good, very comforting thing. She just wasn't sure there would ever truly be room for anyone else in the family, especially if that person was seen to be taking Shelby's place.

Noah wasn't surprised that Tess excused herself and slipped out. She had a great sense of knowing when to give someone space, or privacy. He just didn't expect her to leave the house and go down to the stable, at two in the morning.

"Everything okay?" Noah asked when she came back in.

Lucy had barely had a few sips of her milk before she was fast asleep again. As was Tank.

Now, only he and Tess were fully awake.

Problem was, they were no longer alone in the house, so he couldn't do what he really wanted. Which was to take her back to his bed and make love to her, and sleep with her wrapped in his arms all night long.

Tess's hair was in gorgeous disarray, her cheeks

pink from the cold. Still in her pajamas, she slipped off her coat and rubber boots, and left both in the mudroom. Only her vet bag came into the kitchen with her. She answered his question quietly, with her usual cheerfulness. "Yeah, I just figured as long as I was up…that I'd go out and see how Miss Coco and Baby were doing. And they are both fine."

He searched her face. Aware that sometimes, like now, he had a little trouble reading her. One thing he did know—she seemed to have her guard up again. "You weren't irritated with Lucy's middle-of-the-night house call?"

Tess blinked, looking confused by his query. "No, of course not. Why would you…oh—" She splayed a hand across the center of her chest. Recognition lit her pretty eyes.

"You said it was one of your pet peeves in your previous job."

She slid onto a stool opposite where he was standing. Sighed. "That's true."

He took the saucepan off the stove and poured warm vanilla milk into two mugs. Thinking he might have unintentionally embarrassed her, he continued, "Which is understandable if people were deeming a nothing burger an emergency, and just calling you out, for the sake of calling you out."

Tess sighed ruefully. "Because they were rich and they could? Yeah—" she let out a little breath as their hands touched when he handed her the mug "—that part still rankles and always will. But," she admitted, her voice laced with joy, "I just realized tonight that things are different here. I love the people in Laramie County, and how much they love their pets. The way no one ever throws their weight around. But instead, is helpful and considerate to the max. And, best of all…" She took a long sip of her vanilla milk. "Lucy's a sweetheart."

Aware Tess really seemed to mean that, Noah chuckled. "Are we talking about my moodiest, most demanding child?"

"That would be the one. And actually, I kind of like how she shows her emotions so readily." She flashed him a grin. "You never have to worry where you stand with her. She lets you know, flat-out."

All of a sudden, he felt a little choked up. "She does love you, you know."

"I love her, too." Tess stopped, as if realizing what she had said. She averted her eyes and sipped her milk again. "You know…" She lifted her hand in an airy wave, still not looking at him. "As a family friend."

Funny, he had been thinking, *hoping*, it was more than that. But sensing she needed reassurance things weren't moving too fast, or getting too serious, he said, "Same for Lucy." Even though the intuitive-dad part of him felt like it might be getting to be more than that. A wanting-a-mom-again kind of more.

An introspective silence fell.

He waited for a signal from her. Did she want to head on up to the guest suite? Stay there and talk? He noted with relief it was the latter.

"Anyway," Tess said, turning the conversation back to the subject at hand, "what happened tonight made me realize that what seemed like a pain to me in my old practice was now something I really want to do."

He walked around the island and took the stool next to her. "And that troubles you?"

She shifted to face him. "A little. I thought my stance on that had been in response to my old clients' narcissistic attitudes, but maybe I have my own bit of reckoning to do. Maybe…because of the way I was hurting over the whole Carlton thing…and the really disappointing way it ended…the fact that I knew deep down all along I shouldn't have been letting him make all the decisions but instead should of just stood up for what I wanted and needed, too—I let the situation at work become too much of a battle of control, instead of what was best for the pets and the people who loved them."

Noah could see that. He hadn't been the easiest person to be around when Shelby'd passed, either.

Still, he didn't want Tess to be too hard on herself. Their knees were touching. He could feel the warmth of her legs through her flannel pajama pants. "You are so sweet, you know?"

"But I know I can be aloof, too, especially when I am hurting."

"We all can. And that's okay, too," he continued gruffly.

She gave him a faint half-smile, as if guessing where he was going with this. "Because we're human."

He nodded. "And not perfect. Nor do we have to be."

She took a moment to consider that. Seeming to

not quite agree. He took both her hands in his, wondering if their romance was going to take fire as much as he hoped, when she moved into her own place and they finally had the opportunity to really pursue each other.

For a moment, it seemed like she wanted to kiss him as much as he wanted to kiss her. But then he felt something shift inside of her and he caught the look of wariness filling her eyes.

She was still afraid he would hurt her in the end.

When that was the last thing he would ever want to do.

She slipped off the stool and moved away predictably, her guard up once again. "You're a pretty good guy, too," she returned casually, turning her back on him and picking up her vet bag. "But—" she hitched in a breath "—as you told Lucy, tomorrow's a school day, and a workday, and we all need to get some shut-eye."

Leaving him to ruminate on that, she headed up the stairs and to the guest room.

"Looking at slides already?" Sara asked Tess, early Monday morning.

It was barely seven o'clock, and they were the first two in.

Tess adjusted the microscope, zooming in on the samples she had taken from Tank's ears. "Yep," she said, passing up the chance to admit it was her unwillingness to see Noah that had her here this early.

He might not know it, but she had come very close

to making love with him again last night. And while maybe initially, their intimacy had been a physical release, and a cure for the ever-present loneliness she had felt for some time, now it was getting to be much more than that.

The fact that her heart was involved—with him and his kids—made her way too vulnerable.

And it scared her.

Sara slipped on her white lab coat over the dark blue clinic scrubs the entire staff wore. "What are you seeing?" She sat down at one of the computers and logged in.

Tess frowned. "Just what I thought. Bacteria and yeast in both ears." She grabbed her laptop and added the results to his chart.

Her eyes still on the computer screen in front of her, Sara asked mildly. "Those from Tank Lockhart?"

Tess swiveled around in her chair, curious. "How did you know?"

Sara got out her cell phone. "I got a text from Noah this morning. It said—" she paused to bring the message up, then read "'—go easy on Tess this morning. Tank and Lucy gave her a rough night.'"

Actually, it had been the way Noah had been looking at her, like he wanted to get way more involved with her, that had kept her awake. She wasn't surprised by their physical attraction to each other. But she was a little shocked, and let's face it, thrilled, by the increasing emotional bond developing between them.

A closeness that now had spread to his children.

Angelica, Avery and Lucy were not only coming to rely on her, but they also seemed to love spending time with her as much as she adored spending time with them.

Briefly, Tess explained how Lucy had come to her in concern over her pet. "Although why Noah would think you would need to know about that baffles me." She exhaled and shook her head.

Sara chuckled. "He's just being protective of you, in that gallant way all men are when they are interested in a woman. Which—" Sara's eyes sparkled with hope "—is nice to see."

If it were to last, yes. Which they did not know yet if it would. "Let's not get ahead of ourselves here," Tess said, sensing even more matchmaking to come.

"And let's not lag too far behind, either," her boss teased.

Luckily, several more members of the clinic staff walked in. As well as a client whose cat had gotten into a fight with a possibly rabid raccoon. The rest of the day was packed with a similar mix of appointments and emergencies that kept her thoroughly challenged and busy.

She was happy and exhausted at day's end, when Noah called via FaceTime.

She picked up her cell, unable to stop herself from smiling when she saw his face. Tingles of awareness swept through her. "What's up?"

"The kids want to come into town and have dinner at the Dairy Barn. We were all hoping we could talk you into joining us. See?" He turned the phone and the girls all giggled and pressed their palms together.

"Please!" they yelled in unison.

Tess couldn't help but grin. "You're sure I won't be intruding?"

"Actually," Noah said, turning the camera back to him, "I think it's the other way around. But seriously, they have the best fast food in town."

She returned his confident grin. "So I've heard."

"Problem is…all they have is counter service there."

Like she cared where they ate if she got to spend more time with him and his three adorable daughters. Feigning shock, she splayed a hand across the center of her chest and joked, "Are you telling me I'd have to wait on myself *and you-all, too*?"

He waggled his eyebrows in a way that promised fun, and more fun. "I'm saying I'll pay," he corrected wryly, before he sobered and said, "But you would be required to be an extra hand. Because, well…let's just say when they carry their own trays—" his voice dropped a confidential notch "—it isn't pretty!"

"Daddy!" Lucy chided in the background.

Noah chuckled again. "What do you say, Tess? The kids love it there, and it'll be fun."

The fatigue from a long day faded. She smiled warmly. "Then count me in."

Noah and the girls were waiting for her when she arrived. They ordered burgers, milkshakes and fries. The kids all ate a surprising amount. Tess and

Noah polished off their meals, too. "Do you love it here, too?" Angelica asked, looking around at the old-fashioned ice-cream-shop vibe. The five of them were sitting in a cozy corner booth, centered by a round table.

"'Cause we all do," Avery chimed in.

"I do." Tess smiled.

She frowned as her phone chimed. "Sorry, I have to get this. I'm on-call tonight." She eased away from the table. When she returned, her emotions were crazily awhirl. Noah lifted a questioning eyebrow at her. "Got to go?"

Not quite yet. But soon, she would definitely be leaving her current arrangement. Tess shook her head. "That was the rep from the moving company. She wanted to let me know that the truck will be loaded tomorrow, and here in approximately eleven to thirteen days, depending on the weather."

Clearly, Noah didn't see what the problem was. And Tess knew she shouldn't see one, either.

His mouth quirked. "That's what you wanted, right? For your stuff to get here weekend after next? Right around the time your house is going to be finished and ready to move in?"

Tess nodded. He was right. This was happy news. Then why did she feel so sad?

"Tess is moving?" Avery looked confused. So did her twin.

"Yes, we told you that, remember?" Noah gathered up the trash and began stacking it on trays. "That she was only going to stay with us until her place was ready and her stuff got here."

His matter-of-fact pronouncement was as practical as he was. So how come, Tess wondered, did it leave her feeling disappointed?

"*Where* is your house?" Lucy asked, her brow furrowed.

Grateful for the activity, Tess got up to help clean up, too. She pushed aside her unprecedented emotions. "About five minutes from here. About ten blocks from downtown. On Spring Street."

"Can we go see it? Please?"

Noah looked torn. Their glances meshed. She knew by the way he delayed answering that he was leaving the decision up to her and would back her, either way.

The girls still looked confused and off-kilter. So maybe what they all needed here was a reality check, Tess mused. She forced a brilliant smile. "Yes, of course, we can all go over and take a peek. But we will have to be careful when we walk through it because it's not finished yet."

Scowling, Lucy walked through the downstairs, then the upstairs. Counting rooms under her breath and muttering insults as she went. "It's too small. There is only one bathroom up here."

"We have a powder room downstairs," Tess said.

"And three bedrooms." One of which was going to be a study.

The eight-year-old pivoted, hands planted defiantly on her hips. "It needs to be bigger, like at the Welcome Ranch, where everyone has their own bedroom and bathroom. So," she proclaimed, lifting her chin autocratically, "you need to sell this house and continue staying at our house, with us."

Her suggestion obviously pleased her younger sisters. Angelica yanked on Noah's arm. She smiled hopefully. "We have room, don't we, Daddy?"

With an enthusiastic nod, Avery chimed in, "Yes. Tess can stay with us some more."

For a moment, Noah's expression was inscrutable.

Tess realized this was what he had feared all along. That his daughters wouldn't be able to handle it if they got too close to her, and then she left.

Guiltily, she realized she and Noah never should have lost sight of this. But they had, so...

He hunkered down to face his kids. "Tess knows she is always welcome to stay with us, whenever, however long she wants," he told them all gently.

And Tess knew he meant it. That he would never kick her out or ask her to leave.

Noah gestured at their half-finished surroundings. "But this is her house and she wants to live here with all her stuff. As her friends, we need to all be supportive of that."

Friends...

Was that all she and he were?

Somehow, it had felt like more.

Much *more.*

"Well, I still don't like the house!" Lucy said, fuming.

Avery and Angelica looked at Tess, then their dad,

and back at Tess. "It's very pretty," Angelica said. Then the twins came forward to give Tess a group hug, which she returned.

"We love it," Avery added diplomatically even though it still wasn't finished, and Tess doubted the three-year-olds could envision what it would look like when it was.

The twins gazed up at Tess hopefully. "Can we come and visit you here?" Avery asked.

Tess could feel Noah's eyes on her. His emotions were as deliberately contained as her own.

He gave a slight nod, granting permission.

She ignored the wrenching of her heart, and said, "Anytime it is okay with your daddy, yes, you can."

The rest of the evening and the next day passed swiftly. Tess was called out to a ranch on the other side of the county to care for a pair of calves who'd gotten wound up in a barbed-wire fence and needed stitches. By the time she got home Tuesday evening, everyone was in bed except Noah. He took one look at her exhausted state, and handed her the sandwich and icy cold beer he had waiting for her. She inhaled both, then pointed in the direction of the stairs. "I'm sorry. I don't mean to be rude, but if I don't shower and go to bed soon, I'll never make it up those stairs."

He grinned. "In which case, I would have to carry you. But…unless there is something else you need, we'll say good night now, and meet for brunch in the morning. That's still on, isn't it?"

Even though she knew it might not last, she lived for their Wednesday mornings alone. "It is."

"Then my advice to you," he said, bringing her close for a warm, welcoming hug, before brushing his lips tenderly across her temple, and ever so reluctantly, letting her go, and stepping back, "is sleep in."

Tess tried to, but the girls got in a fight over hair elastics and bows, and the wrong kind of braids, before school. Hearing the ruckus, she felt obliged to go out and help.

Lucy used the time with Tess to lobby. Which, although not surprising, was not the best way to start off a morning.

Luckily, they were already running late. With an exasperated look sent her way, Noah ushered them out the door.

Tess had barely enough time to gulp a quick cup of coffee and get dressed. She had just finished doing her hair and makeup when Noah returned from dropping them off at school.

He lounged in the doorway to her suite. "I'm sorry. Lucy is still campaigning for you not to move out."

Tess moved toward him, not sure this was the best place to have a serious conversation. He closed the remaining distance between them in two steps. Tess could feel his body heat and breathed in the fragrance of mint and man. Wistfully, she let her gaze rove over his solidly built frame and powerful shoulders.

Ignoring the shimmer of sexual attraction between them, she touched his arm sympathetically. "You don't have to apologize, Noah. I know Lucy is at an age where she wants what she wants when she wants it."

The way I am beginning to…

"She's not old enough to have figured out life doesn't always work that way," she added.

Noah looked down at her, his expression still shuttered.

"She will."

Another thoughtful moment ensued. She slipped her hand in his.

He brought her arm up, and for a moment she thought he was going to kiss the inside of her wrist, but then he dropped it back down to her side. A surprising jolt of disappointment went through her.

He shook his head in silent remonstration, looking even more somber now. "It's deeper than that."

Her pulse pounding, Tess waited.

Noah put his arms around her waist and settled her against him. He inhaled sharply. "As you know, we haven't had a woman in the house with us, the way you've been in the house with us, since Shelby died. Honestly, I had gotten so used to being a single parent I didn't think I missed it. But then," he murmured in a tone that seemed to come from the depths of his soul, "you came along, made me see…" He sifted his hands through her hair, lifting her face to his. "That I did."

He kissed her again, as if the need to make her his, not just now, but forever, was stronger than ever. Passion swept through Tess, along with the realization that this need they felt, the connection they'd forged, was something to be treasured.

So what if there were no guarantees where any of this would end, once she moved out, and into her own place in town? He touched and kissed her as if he never wanted their mutual affection to end. And the truth was, neither did she.

Skin heating, desire running riot inside her, she guided him backward to the still rumpled covers on the guest-room bed.

"I want you naked," he growled, taking off her shirt, then her bra and jeans. She kicked off her panties, and he bent her backward, her weight braced against his arm. His lips toured her throat, the curve of her shoulder. The jutting arousal of her nipples, the curves of her breasts and the valley in between.

She watched languidly as his lips closed over the aching crowns. Suckled her gently, lovingly, as if this chance might never come again.

Tenderly caressing her stomach with the flat of his hand, his palm moved lower. She caught her breath as he found her there. She had never felt this beautiful, sensual. Ready.

Moaning softly, she kissed him back while silken brushes of his fingertips alternated with the erotic rubbing of his palm.

Her knees weakened.

She swayed.

Before she knew it, she was coming apart in his arms.

His breath hot and rough against her mouth, he held her until the quaking stopped.

Tess smiled. "My turn, cowboy..."

She undressed him wantonly. A minute later, he joined her naked on the bed.

Indulging in her most secret fantasies, she traced every sinewy inch of him. Lingering over his strong, masculine heat, she kissed her way down the treasure trail, finding him just as hard and ready as she wanted him. Over and over, she kissed and caressed him, taking her time, guiding him deeper and deeper into a vortex of pleasure, until he could take it no more.

Together, they rolled on a condom.

He shifted over her, cupping her hips, lifting them, making them one. Possessing her with a slow, sensual rhythm, he merged their bodies as intimately as they had already begun merging their lives. Until there was nothing but this wild yearning, this incredible passion, this overwhelmingly tender connection.

And this incredible moment in time.

Afterward, they clung together. Their bodies tangled in the covers, neither of them wanted to move.

Noah left a string of kisses in her hair. "I can't believe we just have a little more than a week and a half now, where we'll both be here...under the same roof," he said on a regretful sigh.

Which meant, if they were lucky, one more Wednesday morning just like this.

"Me, either," Tess murmured, cuddling closer. She shut her eyes, drinking in the essence that was him.

But she also knew they had better get used to it. The end date of their arrangement was getting here fast. And like it or not, they were going to have to deal with it.

And then figure out how to move on.

Hopefully, *together...*

Chapter Fifteen

"Well, what do you think?" Molly asked late Thursday afternoon, in full contractor mode.

It had been eleven days since Tess had given Noah and his daughters the tour. A lot had been in-flux that day, the interior only partially done. Now, the entire house was gorgeous, from floor to ceiling.

"I love it." Tess paused to survey the kitchen with the new island, which would provide the culinary prep space she needed, without taking up too much floor space. Unfortunately, it was only big enough for three stools. Which was likely something else Lucy would complain about.

She smiled, thinking how much she enjoyed coaxing Noah's eldest out of her mercurial moods. Helping her feel upbeat and positive again.

Hopefully, the sensitive little girl would come to

see Tess's moving out as something that would not affect their closeness in any way.

"Everything looks magnificent. You and Chance have truly outdone yourselves." She got out her checkbook and paid the balance due upon completion.

Molly pocketed it with thanks. "When will your belongings get here?"

"It's guaranteed to be here anywhere between the thirteen and the sixteenth. Although, right now they are expecting the truck to be here Saturday morning."

"The fourteenth."

Valentine's Day.

Hoping the other woman wouldn't make something of that, Tess nodded. "Yep."

Molly smiled, politely avoiding that minefield. "I bet you'll be glad to get your things so you can finally begin really settling in."

The only problem was she was *already* settled in. At the Welcome Ranch. Not that she hadn't known this day was coming. By Saturday, this house would be her new home. Her reason for staying with Noah and the girls, Tank, Miss Coco and Baby would be gone.

Her heart ached already. She was going to miss them all so much.

And while she would see them as much as she could, it just wouldn't be the same.

Oblivious to Tess's ambivalence, Molly handed over the instruction booklets and warranties for the new HVAC, gas fireplace inset, water heater and kitchen appliances. "Let us know if you have any issues."

"Will do," Tess promised.

Molly left and Tess headed out shortly thereafter. It was nearly dinnertime when she arrived at the ranch. The girls were all seated at the kitchen table, making out their cards for the Valentine's party the next day at school. The twins could each write their own names, on the card, along with little hand-drawn hearts, but needed help addressing the envelopes, so Tess sat down to help with that.

"Where are the candy hearts, Daddy?" Lucy asked.

Noah produced a bowl of pastel candies, with sweet, sentimental sayings on them. The girls began adding them to the cards they had already put in the envelopes.

With a smile, he brought Tess a glass of her favorite blackberry lemonade on ice. Their fingers brushed briefly as he handed it to her. Her stomach vibrated with butterflies. His gaze drifted over her face, lingering on her lips before returning to her eyes.

Warmth crept from the center of her chest, to her cheeks. How much longer were they going to keep their mutual attraction private?

Neither of them was any good at pretending.

Luckily, the girls were so busy finishing up their cards, they did not notice the free-flowing intimacy between them.

"Is there anything I can do to help with meal prep?" Tess asked.

Noah got the salad out of the fridge. "Thanks. I've

She dropped lingerie into the machine. Some of which he had seen her in. Memories of their love-making flooded in, overwhelming her. Her face heating, she turned to face him, hoping he would ignore the slight catch in her breath. "I've loved being here."

He came all the way into the laundry room, soundlessly shutting the door behind him. He clasped her shoulders, gazing down at her.

She cocked her head at him, sensing a building emotion in him, too.

He lifted a hand to her face and rubbed his thumb across the curve of her cheek. "I'm not sure how we're going to get along without you."

She savored the warmth of his touch. His nearness sent her pulse racing. She splayed her hands across the hardness of his chest. "I'm sure you will manage."

He stroked a hand through her hair. With a hand on her spine, he brought her in even closer. He chided softly, "Being *able* to do something and *wanting* to do something are two different things."

How well she knew that! She forced herself to be as practical as they all needed her to be. "True, but Noah...we knew this day was coming. And I really do need to get back in my own place."

"I know." He brushed his lips across her temple. Straightening, his eyes solemn, he assessed her, and in that moment, was full of the same need she harbored. With a sexy half smile, he reminded her, "We also promised each other a real grown-up dinner date when that did happen."

She knew. Boy, did she ever know. She'd been day-dreaming about it ever since he first brought it up.

He shrugged offhandedly. "Given that your stuff is being delivered on Saturday morning…"

Valentine's Day.

She put up a hand before he could continue. She knew from work that everyone had big plans with their love interests or spouses. Here in Laramie County, and San Angelo as well. "We can't go out on the evening of Valentine's Day. Not without attracting a whole lot of unwelcome attention and risking that it would somehow get back to the girls at school."

His lips thinned. "I know," he told her soberly. "I don't want that, either. *When* they hear it, they need to hear it from us."

When, not if…

A thrill surged through her.

Maybe like her, he was beginning to be more serious than either of them had so far admitted.

Serious enough that this relationship could really go somewhere.

"Which is why I was thinking," he continued, taking her by the hand and walking with her out into the kitchen, "maybe we could push our celebration up a day. Go out tomorrow night, after the kids are asleep. Jillian has already agreed to babysit for us."

"So your sister knows?"

"That I want this to go somewhere? Yes, she does. And she is delighted for both of us. Although—" he paused to exhale and roll his eyes "—she had a few choice remarks to make…about me asking you out for a first real date on Friday the thirteenth."

Tess couldn't help but laugh. She hadn't considered that, either. "Good thing I'm not superstitious."

"Me, either." He reached into a bowl of valentine candy and handed her a pink heart that said *Crazy 4 U.* And then another classic that she recalled from when she was a kid. *Be Mine.*

He gazed over at her, his eyes sparkling with sexy mischief. "So what do you say?"

Tess knew she was putting her heart on the line here. She also knew there was only one decision that would not come with immediate regret. Easing away from him with a wink, she murmured, "I'll let you figure it out." She plucked two candies out of the bowl on the table. Handed the first to him.

"*UR Cute,*" he read. "Awww. I like that."

She gave him a second candy.

"*XOXO.* Like that even better," he teased in the gruff but sexy voice she loved so much.

They gazed at each other with pleasure, aware they were definitely at some sort of tipping point. "So your answer is…?" he countered softly.

She stood on tiptoe, wreathed her arms around his neck and brushed her lips against his. "Yes."

"Where is Tess?" Avery asked the next morning, when she came down for breakfast.

"Did she already go down to the stable?" Angelica queried.

It had been their routine to go down for a quick

visit together every morning. And a longer one every evening.

"She had to go to work so she checked in on Miss Coco and Baby on her way out."

"But it's so early!"

Noah handed the girls their farm jackets and rubber boots. He grabbed his own, too. "I know. Sometimes animals get sick in the middle of the night." Together, they headed out. "This time it was the alpacas on the Primrose Ranch. A couple animals were sick and they needed to get a handle on it quickly so the entire herd of them wouldn't become ill."

The twins readily accepted Tess's absence as necessary. Caring for ill animals was her job, after all. Lucy, however, was sanguine about it. Maybe because she'd come to depend on her cheerful interaction with Tess, at the start and end of most days.

His eldest daughter was still in a little bit of a funk when he dropped her sisters off at preschool. Concerned, Noah headed for the elementary school, a mile away. "Something on your mind, sweetheart?" he asked.

Lucy caught his glance in the rearview mirror. "Yes, Daddy." She sat up straight in her seat. "I want to talk. So can you pull over for a minute?"

Better here, on a side street, than in the drop-off line in front of the school. He did as requested, put the SUV in Park, then took off his seat belt and turned around to face her. It was a little awkward, given the confines of the driver's seat, but since she wasn't big enough to sit in the front passenger seat yet, it was the best they could do. He draped an arm across the front seats. "What's on your mind?"

Their eyes met, but only for a moment. "Are you going to ask Tess to be your valentine?"

Whoa. What? He kept his expression inscrutable. "Why would you think that?"

"Because!" Lucy rolled her eyes in exasperation. "She *wants* you to ask her."

He sort of had, with those candy hearts, and the invitation for their first real date tonight. But Lucy didn't know that. And shouldn't, for now. With Tess's belongings arriving tomorrow, and her moving out, after a fantastic, fun, way-too-short month at the Welcome Ranch, they faced too much change as it was. "No, I did not do that, honey."

Lucy squinted her displeasure. "Well, then," she retorted, "Tess will get mad at you, just like Mommy used to do when she didn't get what she wanted and then she will leave us."

Just like that, bad memories came flooding back. His heart going out to his eldest daughter, because she had witnessed and experienced far too much pain and misery in her first eight years of life, he reached over the seat and reminded gently, "Mommy didn't leave us. Not like that. She went to heaven. You know that."

Refusing to clasp his outstretched hand, Lucy harrumphed loudly and clamped her arms across her chest. "But Mommy said she was going to, lots of times, when she got mad at you, Daddy. I *heard* her talk about divorce!"

More guilt flooded Noah's heart. He withdrew his palm, letting his little girl have her space. "That was just in the heat of the moment. She never meant it."

She made another frustrated sound in her throat. "But she did leave, Daddy." She turned her glare toward the window, as another car drove by.

Knowing Lucy needed a reassuring hug whether she wanted one or not, Noah got out of the SUV, and opened the back passenger door. He slid in beside her, wrapping his arms around his daughter. She tensed at first, but he didn't relent in his expression of love, and after a moment, she sagged against him.

He dropped a kiss on the top of her head. "Mommy didn't leave us on purpose. She had an accident, Luce. She fell and hit her head when she was out on a run with her friends. She didn't plan that. And I can assure you that she did not want that. She loved all of us very much and wanted to be here with you and your sisters to see you grow up." Regardless of the flaws in his marriage, he would always wish that, too.

Looking so much older than her years, and wiser and sadder, too, Lucy unclasped her seat belt. She scooted away from him, still radiating a ton of frustration. "The point is, Daddy, Mommy isn't here. She is in heaven. But Tess is here. And *she* could be our new mommy if you would just ask her to be."

The ironic thing was that deep down Noah wanted to ask her. But after everything they'd both been through, a part of him was hesitant. He also knew it wouldn't be wise to hurry things. Or push Tess, who was already a little skeptical that what they had was just a convenient fling.

He knew it was more.

That it had always been more.

From the very first moment they had kissed, and made love.

He also knew Tess deserved the kind of romantic courtship he had never given any woman, including his late wife. Which meant if he wanted their relationship to get off on the right footing, and become as serious and lasting as he wanted, he couldn't act impulsively.

"Lucy," he said gently, trying again. "We just met Tess. I know it kind of feels like she is already part of our family…"

His little girl exhaled with increasing annoyance. "Daddy, Tess is a part of our family! Or she could be if you would just stop being so hardheaded and ask her!"

Hardheaded was what Shelby used to accuse him of being when she didn't get what she wanted.

It hurt to hear his daughter say it, and worried him, too. It was yet more proof he hadn't done enough as a parent, to show her better, more positive ways to resolve conflict.

He would have to get on that. Sooner, rather than later.

"It's a lot more complicated than that," Noah reiterated gently but firmly.

Lucy sighed and turned away.

He knew nothing further was going to be gained

right now, so he opened the door and said, "We can talk about this more this weekend, if you want."

Lucy just huffed out another breath and shook her head.

Hoping she would cool down, with time, he put the SUV back in gear and drove her to school.

"Good news!" Lisa, the clinic receptionist, told Tess at four that afternoon. "Your movers are here!"

Tess put down the chart of the patient she had just seen. The cute Border collie and his owner were now checking out.

"That sounds promising!" Mrs. Brantley said.

Trying not to think about the secret first date she was supposed to have with Noah a few hours from now, Tess smiled back. "It does. Except..." She paused and tried not to frown. "The driver and the guy that's supposed to help him unload weren't supposed to arrive until tomorrow morning."

"That's what they said!" Lisa handed over the message slip she had written out, with the driver's name and number. "But they got here early."

A good seventeen hours early. Which was coincidentally all the time she had left at the Welcome Ranch. "Where are they now?" Tess asked. "Did they say?" She wondered if they would be amenable to taking the evening off. Not that she should even be thinking such a thing. Where were her priorities? With the man of her dreams, of course...

"They did say!" Lisa beamed. "The truck is parked in front of your house. And here is the very best part! They can start unloading for you as soon as you get over there to unlock the door and show them where everything goes."

Sara walked up and joined in the conversation. She began to shoo Tess toward the door. "Go."

"But..." Tess protested.

"We all know how long you have been waiting to get your things. Really, it's no problem. We will handle the last couple of patients of the day."

It didn't seem like she had a choice but to go.

Maybe this would ultimately end up giving her more time to spend with Noah and the girls, over the weekend. Especially if she invited the four of them over to help her unpack...

Unfortunately, it was going to totally screw up the evening she and Noah had planned for themselves as sort of an early Valentine's Day celebration.

Leaving the reception area with a wave goodbye, Tess went to get her things and slipped out the service door. Still trying not to feel too overwhelmed, she called Noah on the way out to her car.

Catching him just as she slid behind the wheel, she explained what had transpired. "So I guess our plans to drive to San Angelo for dinner are kaput."

"That's okay, darlin'. We'll have a rain check as soon as we can work it in next week," he said affably. "It'll be easier to go out clandestinely then, anyway."

Tess closed her eyes and took a deep breath. "Thanks for being so understanding."

"Always," he said in the deep, gruff voice she loved. The one that warmed her through and through.

"Listen, I can still come over later tonight, after Jillian gets here, if you want."

Just like that, the clouds began to part, and she felt the sunshine coming in once again.

She could feel Noah smiling in the silence.

"In the meantime, what can I do to help?" he asked gently.

She was going to need something other than scrubs and a white veterinary doctor's coat to wear this evening. Plus her toiletries, makeup and perfume, all of which were already packed up, ready to go, too.

"I was wondering if you could bring the two suitcases from the guest-room closet into town, when you pick up the girls from school and drop them off."

There was a significant pause. Then he asked, "Sure you don't want to stay here one more night?"

She did. That was the problem. She also knew she needed a reality check before she let her dreams get the best of her.

This was the way things were going to be. She needed to get used to it.

Like it or not, so did Noah.

She forced herself to stay positive. "Um. No. I really need to start unpacking."

There was another silence, a little longer this time. "I understand," he said. Even though he kind of sounded like he didn't. "I'll be there within the hour," he promised.

"Thanks." Trying to tell herself this was indeed no big deal, and she and Noah would adjust to being under separate roofs, as readily as they adjusted to being under the same one, Tess hung up and headed for her home.

The big truck was indeed parked out front. As she stepped out of her Tahoe, she saw the two movers were seated on her front porch, ready to get going.

Tess unlocked the front door. There were papers to be signed, and then they got started.

Slightly more than an hour later, her queen-size bed and dresser, white sectional sofa and pastel wool rug had all been unloaded when Noah parked his SUV in front of her neighbor's home. He had just started up the sidewalk, a suitcase in each hand, when his rear car door, the one closest to the curb, opened up behind him.

Lucy slipped out, her expression mutinous.

The twins were right behind their big sister.

Tess's jaw dropped.

She had assumed he would drop her stuff off before getting the girls at school. Not *after*.

Noah caught the stunned expression on her face, then turned to look behind him just as all three girls dashed past him straight for Tess.

Exasperated did not begin to describe the look on his handsome face. But with both hands full of her heavy bags, there wasn't much he could do except verbally reprimand them. "Girls!" he called after them. "I told you to wait in the SUV!"

Normally, they would have immediately stopped in their tracks and obeyed that deep, paternal tone.

Not this afternoon.

"I want to see what's going on!" Lucy shouted

back, purposely disobeying her dad. She reached the house first and raced up the front steps, right past Tess, and stormed inside.

The twins followed a little less swiftly. "We want to see Tess, Daddy!" Avery explained. Angelica nodded her agreement. Unlike their elder sister, they were more in awe of the big moving truck and all the accompanying activity than upset.

Noah caught up with them as they stopped to gaze around in wonder. Knowing he had them under his supervision, Tess went into the house.

Lucy was stomping around the downstairs in full temper. Tess had never seen her look more miserable. Or scared. And in that moment, she understood as only an orphan could. Lucy had lost her mother. Tess had moved in—temporarily—and started to fill up that void.

Now Tess was leaving, too.

And even though Lucy had known that was the plan all along, she still wasn't ready for the reality of it.

None of them were.

That was abundantly clear when Noah set down her two bags, in the living room, out of the way.

He came toward her, a mixture of sorrow and apology on his face. Like he was hurting, too.

Sensing drama, the movers headed out to the truck.

The twins went to the L-shaped white sofa and sat down, gleefully testing out the cushions, and finding them "very comfy."

Well, at least someone was happy, Tess thought.

Lucy glared at the boxes piled up in the kitchen.

Her face started to crumple. Tess thought she was going to burst into tears. Yet, somehow, she managed to stop her small chin from quavering. "This is all your fault, Daddy!" she said accusingly, crossing her arms in front of her. Her angry eyes filled with tears. "Tess, you need to stop this right now and come back to the ranch!"

"Lucy," Noah warned, his tone stern. "You know better than to be rude. Apologize right now for speaking to Tess like that!"

Lucy shook her head defiantly, still shooting daggers at Tess like she had betrayed them all in the worst way. And maybe she had, she thought miserably. If she'd let the kids think, even for a minute, she could ever fill their mom's place. Never mind know what to do in a volatile situation like this.

Work, animals…she understood.

Family dynamics with multiple kids? Not so much.

"Say you'll come home with us," Lucy demanded again.

Tess knew the child wanted and needed reassurance. But she honestly wasn't sure what to say. Especially since she and Noah were still trying to work things out on their end.

Suddenly, the movers were standing on the porch, ready to bring in Tess's big desk and chair.

Looking exhausted, the taller one asked, "Where do you want this?"

Knowing this was no time for family drama, Tess asked them to put it in the smallest bedroom, upstairs.

Noah ushered his daughters out of the way.

"Tess!" Lucy cried again, plaintively now. The twins slid off the sofa and came to stand beside their big sister. Then, their dad. Their expressions sober and confused, they each hung on to one of Noah's legs, as if abruptly afraid he might go away, too.

"We'll talk about it later," Noah said.

Lucy's distress escalated tenfold.

Tess kneeled down, held out her arms and looked Noah's eldest child straight in the eye. "We will," she promised. But when she tried to give Lucy a commiserating hug, the little girl would have none of it. And she knew when Noah gathered up his girls and shepherded them out of there, that he was every bit as worried as she was.

The movers finished and left at eight thirty on Friday evening. Needing to know how Lucy was doing, Tess texted Noah.

Is Lucy okay?

He wrote back. That's what we need to talk about.

Tess wanted to talk, too, so they could figure out how to handle this together.

I know it's late. Can I come over?

She smiled in relief. Absolutely.

Have you had a chance to eat anything?

That was just like him. So thoughtful. Not yet.

I'll bring something, then.

Thanks. See you soon.

Figuring she had just enough time, Tess opened up her suitcase and got what she needed to freshen up. She had just changed out of her work clothes and into jeans and a sweater when the doorbell rang.

Noah was on the other side of the portal, with a picnic basket full of wine, cheese, gourmet crackers, a loaf of crusty bread and fruit.

He handed over the basket, then went back out to his SUV, returning with a large shopping bag. Inside was a satin heart filled with chocolate candy, a funny Valentine card, asking her to be his forevermore, and a beautiful bouquet of antique red roses from his sister Jillian's ranch.

Stunned, Tess looked at the array of gifts. She was touched by the grand romantic gesture, but wasn't used to being spoiled. And none of this was part of their agreement. She sat back, not sure what to say, except the truth. "You didn't have to do all this, Noah. Especially tonight. Especially after what happened with Lucy."

"I wanted to." He brought her close, kissing her sweetly, deeply.

She curled against him, soaking up his warmth and his strength.

But, eventually, he drew back. "But you're right,"

he murmured, tenderly stroking a hand through her hair. He kissed her cheek, then their gazes met and held. "We do need to talk."

Tess could tell by the careful way he was looking at her this wasn't going to be good.

She also knew there was nothing they couldn't handle as long as they approached it as a team.

Still held safe in his arms, she drew on every ounce of courage she had. She reminded him, "You never answered my text about Lucy."

Sadness came and went in his deep blue eyes. An interminable pause ensued. Finally, he admitted thickly, "She was still upset when I tucked her in."

Tess took in the grim set of his sensual lips. "How upset?"

He eased away, his every step crackling with deliberately suppressed emotion. "She pretty much cried herself to sleep." Shoulders slumping, he turned to look at the flames licking at the gas-log inset. He shook his head in regret, then swung back around. "I did my best to comfort her, but she wasn't having any of it."

Guilt mixed with shame, that she had somehow made such a mess of things with his sweet, sensitive, passionate-to-a-fault, eldest child. "I'm sorry." She took a seat on the sofa and motioned for him to do the same. "I never meant for this to happen."

Accepting her rueful look with a nod, Noah exhaled. He took a seat beside her, opened up the bottle of pinot noir and poured two glasses.

Maybe eating something would help them both feel better.

Using the plates and utensils he had provided, she sliced cheddar, gruyere and gouda. Spread out an array of crackers, too.

Tess admitted sadly, "If I'd had any idea that she would react to my leaving, the way she did today..."

"I know that." Broad shoulders tensing, he sipped his wine. "Which doesn't mean that I shouldn't have seen it coming." He gripped his glass with both hands, staring down into the liquid. "I knew Lucy was still struggling with her grief over losing her mom. I thought moving back here, spending time with her cousins and aunts and uncles, and living on a ranch, would help her move on."

Sensing he needed his physical space, more than a hug, Tess sipped her wine, too. "But she hasn't."

Noah swung to face Tess, his bent knee bumping up against hers. "I thought she was. Especially by the way she had started to accept you—i.e., another woman who wasn't her mom—in our lives."

Tess held back a frustrated sigh. "But now she thinks I—*we*—betrayed her."

Noah's expression grew even bleaker. "She really did not want you to leave."

Tess really hadn't wanted to leave, either. But she also knew she and Noah couldn't just jump into a long-term, lifelong relationship the way he had with his ex, on the spur of the moment, and expect everything to magically work out. Not when his kids and their emotions were involved. Because he was right—he and his girls had already lost too much.

She could see he was struggling with the complexity of the situation. "So what do you think we should do?" she asked gently. Because like it or not, this involved both of them.

He put aside his glass of wine and stared at the food as if he had zero appetite. "Not entirely sure."

Nor was she.

"But," he said, picking up a slice of cheese and a cracker, and holding it like it was kryptonite, "I am going to put Lucy back in a grief group for kids, like the one she was in back in California. And maybe go to counseling with her, too."

That sounded like a positive step. Encouraged, Tess smiled, "Do you want me to go to that, too?"

"No." He put the cheese and cracker on a napkin, next to his barely touched pinot noir. He kept his glance averted. "I don't think that will be necessary."

Tess couldn't say why exactly. Maybe it was his cool, pragmatic tone, or the fact he wouldn't look her in the eye, but it felt like she had just been shoved to the side and had a door slammed in her face.

"Is that because I'm the problem? That, or the way I've dealt with things? Letting Lucy and I get too close, too soon?" *Letting us feel like we could be mother and daughter one day?* Heart aching, Tess pushed on deliberately, "Or is it because you don't want to give her the mistaken idea that I'm ever going to be there for her again, the way I have been recently?" *Because you are not really sure that I will be? Especially if my presence makes your life more complicated, instead of just easier.* There was no way to tell for sure. She only knew he suddenly had reservations, about them moving forward as the tight knit team they had become over the last weeks. And that reaction made her think of her ex. The small but deliberate ways Carlton had started extricating himself from her, before they split up for good. She didn't think she could bear that kind of pain again. Noah didn't look as if he wanted to suffer that way, either, which was why he was probably starting to put up a wall around his heart, again.

The silence drew out, even more painfully. Clearly still struggling emotionally with all this, Noah let out a long breath. He turned to her once again. "I'm not trying to hurt you, Tess."

But he was nevertheless, she thought miserably.

He swallowed. "I don't want you to be part of our counseling process, because I feel like this is a problem that Lucy and I have to solve separately, apart from you."

And just like that, Tess was inundated with memories of other times when she had been excluded, and pushed aside, only to ultimately end up alone. Now, she *really* felt like crying.

"But that doesn't mean you and I still don't have work to do to provide a solid foundation for what happens next," he told her soberly.

Now he had really lost her. She bit her lip. Sensing he was about to say something he really wished he did not have to say, she said, in return, "I don't understand."

He leaned a fraction closer, inundating her with his heady masculine essence. "I know it might seem like it is too soon for me to ask you this, given everything that has gone on today." He took her hand in his, stroking the palm of her hand with the pad of his thumb.

Delicious sensations swept through her.

The kind that usually preceded making love.

His eyes turned a molten blue. "And I don't want you to be pressured into saying yes." He gripped her hand tighter. "But—"

The last thing Tess wanted was any kind of proposal born out of despair. Panicked, she withdrew her hand from his. Stood and went over to adjust the flame on the gas fireplace.

She knew she shouldn't have interrupted him at that crucial moment. But she couldn't help it. She didn't want them going down another path they never should have begun. She swung back to him. "If you're having this much reservation, then maybe we really shouldn't talk about it yet." Just like maybe they shouldn't have rushed into acting on their fierce physical attraction to each other and making love.

Her plea for caution fell on deaf ears.

No less determined, he walked over to stand next to her, coming right up to her face. "I want us to be together, Tess." He clasped her shoulders, the tenderness of his hands sending warmth swirling through her. Making her want to forget the talk and simply kiss him. Lose herself completely in the two of them. Worry about all the problems facing them, later.

He leaned forward, too, his expression so earnest and sincere. "But…"

And here it came. The break-up.

Lips tightening, he continued, with obvious regret, "It can't happen the way things are right now." His gaze shifted lovingly over her face. In a way that suddenly seemed to indicate he was as committed to her, as he had been. In a way that said, he still wanted to move forward. As long as she gave him exactly what he asked for…

"Unless we take steps to *really* change things in a positive, permanent sense."

Tess blinked. Was he really about to ask her to forego any kind of courtship and just run off and get married, the way he had with his late wife?

While it might provide the constancy the kids yearned for, as well as the deeply romantic relationship and longevity she had always wanted, a hasty act like that would also add to the overall confusion. Not just for the kids, but for her, too! Because the only reason she had ever wanted to marry was for deep, abiding love and commitment, and that did not happen overnight. It took time.

She thought of Lucy's despair earlier. Knew for all their sakes' she had to get Noah to slow down and take a step back. She lifted a hand in stop-sign fashion. "I agree. The kids need stability. Permanence. And if we can't give that to them right now…" *Or ever, maybe, she worried unhappily, if you're going to start setting conditions for us to be together...*

"Then we have to make adjustments," he agreed.

Reassured they were on the same page, she began to relax. Maybe the thing to do was not pretend she and he didn't feel anything for each other when they did. Wouldn't it be better to just be honest with the kids, at least as far as they were able, and let them know that she and Noah cared about each other. *Deeply.* And build very, very slowly from there.

"Because I don't want to end up in the same situation I did with Shelby."

Not a comparison she wanted made. Especially by him. Beginning to feel like the rug was being pulled out from under her again, she asked warily, "What do you mean?"

His dark eyebrows drew together. "Well, my late wife and I couldn't always get along."

So he had mentioned previously.

"And when we did disagree, we would usually end up arguing." He exhaled, unhappy again, then shoved a hand through his hair. "I'm only now beginning to see just how much those quarrels affected Lucy."

Who was a very sensitive, often introspective little girl who tended to keep her feelings bottled up until they exploded. "But not the twins?"

"They were infants when we lost Shelby. They don't recall anything about her other than what they hear others, mostly Lucy, talk about. And even that, they don't really understand. So none of this is an issue for them. At least not right now. If it becomes one, I'll get them into a grief group, too."

"So what are you trying to ask me, that you can't quite bring yourself to actually say?" she said finally, feeling even more confused. Clearly, this wasn't any kind of a proposal, Tess thought. Surprised to realize that for a moment she had thought—hoped—maybe it was. Even though the supposed rationale behind it and the timing would have been all wrong.

He opened his mouth and shut it. "I want to know if you will hold off on the two of us taking our relationship public indefinitely. And go to couples counseling with me instead."

Couples counseling. The phrase reverberated in Tess's head. Again and again…

Noah watched her react, as if she was a time bomb that could go off at any second. "You look upset."

Duh. Did he think? Deciding this evening had to come to an end, she marched over and turned off the gas fireplace. "I am."

His expression showed his astonishment, and he watched the flame dwindle to nothing. "Why?"

Tess rubbed her forehead, feeling a headache coming on. "Because I've been down this road before, with my ex. He had doubts about whether we belonged together or not from the very beginning, but he couldn't admit that. So every time we got close to taking our relationship to the next level, he put in some new caveat that we would have to abide by."

Noah frowned, impatient. "Like you could spend the

night together, but only once a week, so you wouldn't be distracted from your vet-school studies. Stuff like that," he said, recalling what she'd told him.

She nodded. "And always doing what we each needed to do for ourselves first, like take post residency jobs in other states."

"You think if you hadn't done that the two of you would still be together?"

"No." Tess grimaced, the pain she felt over their failed romance long gone. "I don't. Because all that did was show how wrong we were for each other." The ache in her chest grew, and she gestured helplessly. "Kind of like where you and I are now."

He went still. "Now I'm the one who really doesn't get it."

Her body felt locked up tight. "Then let me spell it out for you, cowboy. If this is where our fling is headed," she warned him, her heart breaking, "I wish you would just have the guts to make a clean break."

"I don't want to end this fling, Tess. I'm here tonight because I want it to work! And I especially want it to work for the kids."

She could see that.

And yet...

Tess's heart ached as she thought how utterly miserable Lucy had been. How unwilling to accept comfort. Much like she felt right now. Maybe she and Noah's eldest daughter were more alike than he knew.

Maybe it was time to be realistic and do what was best for each and every one of them.

Especially his children.

Wearily, she said, "The chivalrous side of you probably does want everything to work out with fairy-tale precision. Because otherwise you would have been using me for sex and vet care and part-time nanny work, just like I apparently inadvertently used you for lodging and sex and the cure to the kind of loneliness you feel when you move to a place where you don't know a soul.

"And you don't want to think of yourself as that kind of guy, any more than I want to think of my-self as that kind of woman. As someone who would trade intimacy for tangible goods and services. Yet, here we are." She shook her head ruefully. "With you trying the most creative way ever to let me down easy. In a way that will ultimately absolve you of any kind of blame."

A muscle ticking in his jaw, he gave her an incred-ulous look. "What are you saying? That you think I'm going to lure you into couples therapy, so some-one else can tell us we are incompatible? And use that as an excuse to end this?"

Well, he *had* said the first night they met he didn't want to date or be married again, that his life was too full as it was. She had told him the same thing. And she had meant it with all her heart, at the time.

Trouble was, living with him and his girls had changed all that for her. She did want a husband and kids. She wanted a *life* with him.

And he, apparently, still wanted a life without a wife. A life on his ranch, with just him, and his girls and their pets.

Which was what made this all hurt so bad. Knowing that he did not need to be with her to be happy.

She shrugged, her emotions getting the better of her once again. "Stranger things have happened."

"Do you really think I would use someone else to break up with you?" He rubbed a hand across the scruff on his jaw and continued harshly, "I'm not that kind of man, Tess. I thought you knew me better than that."

Her heart aching in a way she had never imagined it could, she told him coolly, "I thought I did, but your actions tonight say otherwise." She walked stiffly to the front door, and opened it. "We need to end this," she said. Cold air came streaming in, adding to the discomfort between them. "And you need to leave."

He stared at her in disbelief as she picked up his jacket and shoved it into his hands. His jaw tautened. "So that's a *no* to counseling?"

"A *no* to that," she confirmed sadly, "and anything else you ever ask!"

He put his hands on her shoulders, his touch as soft and compelling as his low voice. "Tess. Please. Don't do this." His voice caught as her heart wrenched in her chest. "You're making a terrible mistake."

Was she? Or was he? Were they both? She only knew one thing.

If he continued holding her, if she surrendered to his warmth and strength, they would end up kissing again, and if they kissed, they'd make love, and she would be in deeper still.

And that, she feared, would destroy her if, in the end, this didn't work out.

"I can't talk about this anymore." She wrenched herself from his grasp.

For a moment, she thought he was going to try and persuade her again.

Then something changed in his face. Went cold and still.

He stared at her a second longer, then turned without a word, and walked right out the door.

Chapter Sixteen

Twenty minutes later, feeling more hurt, and numb, and disappointed than he ever had in his life, Noah walked into his home. His sister was curled on the sofa, reading a book. "Thanks for babysitting," he told Jillian. With the kids asleep, and Tess not there, it had never seemed quieter. Although he supposed in defeat, without Tess there going forward, it would likely feel even more desolate to him. Especially during the times he'd come to depend on spending with her. Early mornings, late nights. Their Wednesday morning lovefests.

He'd been a fool to let himself fall for her.

To think she would ever be able to really let her guard down and open up her heart enough to let him in. Or think that he would be any better at man-woman relationships this time around.

Oblivious to the anger still simmering inside him, Jillian continued surveying him in surprise. "That must have been the shortest date on record. You've only been gone an hour and a half!"

"Good to know." Not up for a heart-to-heart, Noah got his sister's coat. He walked over to hand it to her. "Thanks again for babysitting."

Seemingly aware there was reason for concern, she put up a hand, refusing to be escorted out. "Uh-uh, buddy. I am not leaving until I find out why you have *that look* on your face."

Oh, boy, here they went. "What look?" he asked wearily. As far as emotions went, after his quarrel with Tess, he was all tapped out. Not that this would satisfy his incredibly romantic sister.

She made room for him on the sofa. "The look that says the world has ended. What happened?"

Equally empathetic, Tank got up from his place on the hearth and came over to sit next to Noah, cuddling against him.

He reached down and petted his dog's head. Robotically, he explained, "Tess's furniture arrived today. She has a house full of moving boxes. She wanted it to be an early night, so we cut it short. It's no big deal."

Jillian tilted her head. No doubt thinking about the beautiful bouquet of antique roses she had brought over for him to take to Tess. She'd also seen the wicker basket and shopping bag full of gifts he'd walked out with. And knew a romantic evening had been planned. "Except it looks very much like it *is* a big deal to you," she noted gently. "Did you re-schedule?"

He shook his head.

She surveyed him intently. "Why not?"

Tank turned to look at him, too. "Because Tess never wants to see me again."

"Ah, now the rub... What did you do?"

Her accusing tone rankled. "Why do you assume it's me?" he asked heatedly.

"Because I've spent time with Tess and I know she is not the type of person who overreacts at the slightest thing. Plus, I've seen the way she looks at you when she doesn't realize anyone else is watching. She's in love with you, dude. She's *been* in love with you from that first weekend."

Hope rose only to be immediately quashed. He knew better than anyone that love didn't solve everything. Sometimes passion made it worse. And tonight had definitely been the pits.

"She and I never said anything about love," he said, biting out the words.

"But you were close."

More than that. *Inseparable.* To the point he hadn't been able to imagine his future without her in it. His gut knotted. "I thought so."

Silence.

"What was supposed to happen tonight?" she asked.

"We were going to have our first real date. But we were going to do it on the down-low."

"Because the two of you are still in that private stage of your relationship?"

Was it a relationship? He had thought so. Hell, he had thought it was even more than that. Which just showed how much he knew.

"Yeah, we didn't want anything getting back to the girls until things were more settled. You know how people, especially in our family, can jump to conclusions when it comes to romance."

Jillian shut her book and set it aside. "But you thought things would be more settled soon, so you could start openly dating and tell everyone you were seeing each other, even the kids?"

"That was the plan. At least—" Noah exhaled his frustration "—until Lucy became upset, when she found out Tess was moving out of our guest room, and into her home in town today." Briefly, he told his sister about the conversations he had had with his eldest daughter both before and after school.

Jillian gave a slow, pensive shake of her head. "And that worried you because she is such a sensitive kid."

"Right. Which is why I told Tess that I would be enrolling Lucy in a grief-support group for kids again, and taking Lucy to counseling to help her get through this new wave of grief."

Jillian leaned forward. "Did you ask Tess to be part of that?"

He shook his head, still firm in his decision. "No. I didn't think it was a good idea."

She gave him a baleful stare. "Why not?"

"Because," Noah explained sourly, "if ultimately it

didn't work out between Tess and I, then Lucy would suffer *yet another loss*."

"Lucy... Or you?"

Man, his sister didn't pull any punches. "Both of us," he retorted tersely. "But it's Lucy I am mainly concerned about here."

"Uh-huh."

Jillian didn't believe him.

Noah wasn't sure he believed himself.

Because the truth was, he was now in as much pain and distress as his eldest child had been earlier. As hopeless that things would ever work out again, too.

He grimaced in renewed defeat. Then made himself focus on what he hopefully could fix with love and time. "Back to Lucy...and the loss she could suffer..."

"Could?" Jillian harrumphed. "You don't think she is suffering one now?"

"Not as much as she would be, if she gets her hopes raised only to have them dashed again."

His sister looked at him with perceptive eyes. He could tell she was holding back a whole lot of what she wanted to say. Finally, asking only, in a cool, calm voice, "How did Tess react to this plan of yours?"

"She was okay..."

A raised eyebrow.

"Sort of..." Noah amended. "Until I asked her to hold off on telling anyone we were seeing each other indefinitely, while we went to couples counseling."

This time Jillian was so shocked she nearly fell off the sofa. "You…*what*?"

Noah was getting really tired of defending his plan. Why couldn't Tess and Jillian see he was trying to protect everyone here? Keep them from getting hurt? He met his sister's gaze equably. "I wanted to head off any problems before they arose so we wouldn't make the same mistakes that Shelby and I made."

"So Tess wouldn't make the same errors?" Jillian persisted. "Or *you* wouldn't?"

Noah blinked.

Jillian heaved an exasperated sigh. She looked like she wanted to throttle him. "Tess isn't Shelby, Noah."

"I know that," he said, defending himself stiffly.

Jillian studied him. "Funny thing is, I think you do. So why did you do something that you had to know on some level would end this whatever-it-is with Tess almost before it began?"

Why indeed?

Could it be, Noah wondered, that Tess wasn't the only one with barbed wire around her heart, that he was running from his feelings, and putting up roadblocks to protect himself, too? Had he unconsciously used Lucy's issues as a cover to keep from really acknowledging his own true fear—that he would never be able to love and protect and care for Tess, the way she wanted, needed, and deserved? Was that what was holding them back, and keeping him from going all in with Tess right now?

* * *

Tess was still in a major funk the next afternoon, when Sara stopped by to bring a housewarming gift and see how things were going. "I'm surprised I don't see a whole crew of Lockharts here helping you put everything in order, posthaste."

"Yeah, well, those days are over." Tess accepted the Sugar Love bakery basket with a thanks. "Noah and I probably aren't going to be good friends after all."

Sara followed her into the kitchen. Then watched as Tess set down the present. "I was hoping you were more than that."

So was I, Tess thought, recalling the Valentine's Day presents Noah had brought over—flowers, candy and funny card.

"Did he do something?" Sara asked gently. "Because it doesn't look to me like you wanted to end things."

"I didn't." Briefly, she explained about how close she had gotten to Noah and his kids, while staying at the Welcome Ranch. Plus, Lucy's meltdown the previous day.

Sara sympathized. "I'm sure that was tough on all of you. But Lucy and the twins know they will still see you, right?"

"That was the plan, initially." Tess folded her arms over her chest, over her heart.

"And now?" Sara lounged against the new granite counter.

Tess got out two bottles of sparkling water and

handed one to Sara. "Noah wants to take Lucy to a grief-support group and counseling, and deal with that himself." Together, they walked into the living room and sat on the sofa.

Sara took off her winter jacket and set it beside her. "Even though you are part of the reason she is so upset."

Tess ran her fingertips over the knee of her jeans. "Yes."

"But you accepted that."

The depth of her hurt made her tense. "I did. After all, he is the parent and maybe I shouldn't be involved in this crisis with his daughter." *At least not right now.* "But when he asked me to hold off on telling people we were going to start dating and instead go to couples counseling first, to be sure we were going to be compatible, it became clear to me we weren't on the same page after all."

To Tess's surprise, her boss didn't look at all surprised by Noah's plan.

"The request felt like it came out of left field?" Sara guessed.

"And then some," Tess confirmed, feeling more unsettled than ever.

Sara tilted her head. "And you're opposed to going because you don't like therapy in general? Or because you don't want to go to couples counseling with *him*?"

"I'm opposed because I think his even asking me to do that sends a strong signal that he's gotten more involved with me than he ever wanted to be, or planned on being, and now he doesn't know how to get out of it, with his self-esteem and character intact." She released a long, labored breath. "So he's going to let someone else do the heavy lifting and tell us kindly that we are not a good match after all. And then he won't have to feel guilty or like he led me on when we do split up."

"That's a lot of work just to say he's not ready to date after losing his wife. Which has clearly been the case up to now. Usually, he just tells a woman outright. Politely and directly, so there are no misunderstandings. Which is one of the things that has made it very hard to match him up with anyone."

Tess hadn't been ready or willing to date anyone either, when they had first met. They had both been up front about that.

"But if that were the case," Sara continued, "you are not the kind of woman who would hold his continued grief and unwillingness to move on against him. And I know that he knows that. So he could have just ended it, without all the extra confusion and drama, if that was what he wanted."

Tess buried her face in her hands. Had she been wrong comparing him to Carlton? Thinking he was taking the coward's way out, or putting up roadblocks to prevent them from getting closer? She swallowed. "Then why did he ask me to go to couples therapy with him before we really even had our first official date?"

Sarah flashed a gentle, understanding smile. "The same reason I joined a support group for spouses and asked Matt to get counseling at the West Texas Warriors Association for his PTSD, when the two of us first got emotionally involved. Because I knew without some outside help, our chances to have a healthy family were never going to be as good as we both wanted them to be."

Tess took a moment to think about that.

"There are a few other reasons he would have come up with this solution. First, his mother is a social worker and she is very good friends with Kate Marten McCabe, who runs the grief-counseling services at Laramie Community Hospital. So I am sure she has been wanting him to do this, anyway. Plus, Noah and his family went through a lot of trauma, both when Shelby was in cancer treatment and after she died, and Noah and Lucy both did grief counseling in California that first year."

"He mentioned that," Tess admitted. "He told me that's why they moved back to Texas. So he and the girls could be close to his parents and all his siblings, for the familial support."

"Right." Sara filled in some more gaps in Tess's knowledge. "And although Lucy has continued to struggle from time to time, mostly from sibling rivalry these days, it has seemed like they were all finally moving on. Especially by how they all welcomed you into their lives this last month."

Sara's hopeful analysis made sense. And yet... Tess had behaved foolishly once. She did not want to jump to erroneous conclusions again. "I still think he is looking for a way out, now that I'm no longer going to be living with them," Tess admitted stubbornly.

"Is he?" Sara asked kindly. "Or are you?"

Tess spent the rest of the day unpacking and thinking. Was Sara right?

Was *she* the one who was scared?

By the following afternoon, she knew what she had to do. She developed a plan. Her heart feeling like it was lodged in her throat, she texted Noah.

Are you free tonight? I'd really like to talk.

She saw the little bubbles that indicated he was responding.

What time? he texted back.

Her knees sagged in relief. Seven? My place?

I'll be there.

The next few hours passed with a flurry of activity and anxiety. When the doorbell finally rang, Tess's pulse was racing. Smoothing the folds of her skirt, she went to answer it. Noah stood on the other side, in a cashmere sweater and slacks, looking as handsome as could be.

Her heart took another leap. She ushered him in.

"Wow…" He looked around at the perfectly put-together living room and kitchen. His voice was a sexy rumble in his chest. "Who helped?"

She thought about all the boxes she had emptied

and collapsed and carried out to the garage, for re-cycling. "Just me."

"If you weren't a veterinarian, you could hire out for this." He caught her wry look. "Sorry." He so-bered. "When I'm nervous I make jokes. The place really does look nice."

Pride and contentment radiated within her. "Thank you." She took him by the hand and led him over to the sofa, trying hard not to notice how warm and solid and enticingly masculine he felt. Or how good he smelled, like soap and cologne. They settled side by side. "And for the record, I'm nervous, too."

He gazed at her hopefully. "So…"

"First, I'd like to apologize for kicking you out Friday evening and peremptorily ending our date. I should have had you stay and let us work through this."

He studied her closely, still on edge. "Which means you're willing to do so now?" he asked in a low voice, husky with emotion.

Tess nodded. "I talked to Sara about what the WTWA counseling services had done for her and Matt, how it had made their love so much stronger and better. And I know now I completely overre-acted when you asked me to consider counseling."

He threaded his hand through hers. "Why did you?" he asked gently.

She moved closer. "That took a while to figure out, but eventually I began to put it all together." Their gazes locked. "You remember when I told you that a lot of different family friends cared for me while my mom worked nights at the restaurant?"

"Mmm-hmm." He shifted her over onto his lap and wrapped his arms around her.

"Well, there was always a point when my welcome kind of got worn out. But everyone who cared for me was so kind, no one wanted to see me go without care, and they knew especially in the early days for my mom and me, finances were tight. So the person or family would soldier on, thinking they could do it. Until it became just too hard or inconvenient to have me there."

His gaze remained on hers, as steady and strong as his presence. "And then they would tell you and your mom to find other arrangements?"

Tess sighed ruefully. "If only they had been able to be that direct, maybe it would have been easier. Instead, they started making up excuses as to why they couldn't care for me."

"That you were able to see through."

She nodded, sadness drifting over her. "It was pretty obvious, even at an early age." She released a deep, shuddering breath. His rapt attention encouraged her to go on. "Anyway—" she hitched in another breath "—when you brought up the idea of going to counseling, I thought that was what it was. Again."

His expression remained serious, even as his welcoming smile broadened. "Oh, darlin', the last thing I ever wanted was to push you away," he confessed huskily. His gaze roved her face, lingering on her eyes. "I was just so afraid of making the kinds of mistakes I made in my first marriage." He threaded his hands through her hair, and gazed down at her. Repentantly. Somberly.

"Of hurting the kids again. Hurting you. And I couldn't bear the thought of that," he confessed raggedly.

She splayed her hands over the steady thrumming of his heart. "The only thing we ended up hurting was each other."

"Agreed."

"I want to go to couples counseling with you, Noah. I want to learn how to be the best partner and mother figure possible."

He studied her intently. "You're sure?"

Tess noted with relief, it was no longer a condition for moving forward. "Very." She offered a tremulous smile. "I'm coming late to this party. I want to get started off on the right foot." She caught the happy gleam in his eyes and murmured mischievously, "We'll consider it a kind of imprint training for...us."

Beaming, he took her face in his hands. "I think I could go for that."

"Me, too." She kissed him fiercely.

He kissed her back until they were both breathless and then rested his forehead against hers.

"Oh, Tess, I love you," he told her in a low, rusty sounding voice. "I love you so much..."

They shared another sweet, evocative kiss. Tess wreathed her arms about his neck. "I love you, too,

Noah." Bliss filled her heart. For a long moment, all they could do was drink each other in.

He flashed her a sexy smile. "So we're back on track?"

She met his coaxing look with one of her own. "To a future together? Absolutely."

Epilogue

Lucy propped her hands on her hips, as her little sisters gathered around. "Well, what do you think, Daddy?" She tossed her long hair triumphantly. "Are we beautiful or what?"

Noah stepped back to admire the family in his life on their beloved Welcome Ranch. Tess and the girls had matching spring dresses on. The rose pattern of the fabric was carried over into the wreaths they wore in their hair, and the ribbons attached to the donkeys' halters, as well as to Tank's collar.

They looked so damn fine and were so happy it brought tears to his eyes. The support groups and therapy had provided them with the skills needed to weather any problem, big or small. His and Tess's marriage six months before had provided a testament to their faith in the future, and a solid foundation for their lively family. He surveyed them all in turn, his heart filling with love and pride. "You all are gorgeous!" he told them in a low, gravelly voice. His gaze swept gratefully over Tank, Miss Coco and Baby, too.

They were all so damn lucky to have what they did.

Looking a little choked up as well, by their incredible family, Tess grinned. "We can't forget what Aunt Jillian brought over for you, too, cowboy." She pulled out a matching pale pink-rose boutonniere and pinned it to the lapel of his linen sport coat. She patted his chest while gazing lovingly into his eyes. "You're going to be our master of ceremonies today——" her gaze scanned his open-throated white shirt, jeans and boots "——so you've got to be as dressed up as the rest of us. Right, girls?"

"Right, Mommy!" the three of them declared in return.

Tess beamed, the way she always did when the girls honored her as their new mother. Which wasn't surprising, since she loved them just as fiercely in return. Things hadn't been perfect, of course. They'd all had their ups and downs. But they'd all weathered the storms together, and come out, closer than ever, every time.

Angelica clapped her hands while Avery squealed in excitement. "The Pet Palooza at the fairgrounds is going to be so much fun!"

Noah imagined it would be.

The first annual event had been organized by his wife. All the kids would walk with their parents and leashed pets around the fairground track. Then retire to the pens in the various barns, after the low-key parade, to await their turn on stage, as they introduced their pets and told all about their care.

Everyone who participated would get a trophy for their pet. And there were going to be lots of them.

"Are there going to be any other miniature donkeys?" Lucy asked.

Tess shook her head as they shepherded Miss Coco and Baby to the waiting horse trailer, which had been lined with soft, clean hay. "No, but there will be two Shetland ponies, a lot of lambs and sheep and goats, a few alpacas, a chicken and a rooster, and even some full-sized horses."

Thanks to carefully ordered placement, the parade went great. The time in the pens gave them all an opportunity to relax. When it was their turn on stage, Noah held the microphone and asked the questions of his daughters, about their pets' care and personalities. Tess fielded the veterinary-level inquiries. And Miss Coco, Baby and Tank showed off their charm.

All three were given superior ratings. And, to their delight, the girls each received an award for being such good pet owners.

By the time they all got back to the ranch, they all partook in the picnic dinner they had prepared before they left. It had been a long exhausting, fun-filled day for everyone, and before they knew it, the girls were ready for sleep, all the animals bedded down for the night.

Tess and Noah retired to the newly installed porch swing on the back deck, in time to watch the sunset. He'd thought Tess might want to open a bottle of wine, but instead she had an icy cold beer for him, and a raspberry lemonade for herself.

She settled down into the curve of his arm and clinked her glass with his. "Great job today, Daddy."

"Great job to you, too, Mommy," he teased right back.

They exchanged smiles.

His thoughts turned to the conversation they hadn't had time to have that morning. "Any ideas about what you want to do about the offer on your house?"

She sipped her lemonade serenely. "I'm going to accept it."

He knew the bid had been over asking price. Still… "Are you sure?"

She nodded. "I know I honored my family by returning the property to its former glory, but Lucy was right the first time she did a walk-through with us. It is too small. And we have the home here, on the Welcome Ranch."

He wrapped his arm about her shoulders, drawing her into his body. "It still has sentimental value to you, though."

She rested her head in the curve of his neck. "You're right." She took his hand and pressed it to her lips. Remembering. "It's the place we first met, the thing that brought us together initially, and the place where a lot of our courtship occurred. Where we occasionally have hosted sleepovers for the girls and their friends and or cousins. And had the occasional staycation as well."

All were wonderful memories. His heart swelling with love, he kissed her temple. "It's also where they were the first time they called you Mom."

"I know." Her eyes misted over.

He pushed on, wanting to make sure she would not make a decision that would later lead to regret. "And there's no mortgage on it. Just a small amount of property tax to be paid every year, which is offset by the increase in value. So if you wanted to keep it as an investment, or even a hang-out place for us when the girls are busy in town, I would understand. I mean, who knows, maybe one of the girls would want to live in it one day."

Tess turned to face him, her expression sober. "I thought about that. But that would be years from now, Noah, and the house needs to be occupied now by a loving family, like the one who made the offer. Besides—" she grinned impishly "—when I said the house is too small for us, I really meant it, cowboy."

For a second, he wasn't sure where she was going with this. When she took his hand and put it on her tummy, he began to get the idea. Suddenly, he felt like he'd been picked up by a tornado and set down so hard all the wind was knocked out of him. Yet, somehow, he was still upright. Feelings bubbling up inside of him—joy, love surprise, wonder—and he rasped, "You're…?"

"Pregnant." Her smile was as dazzling as her beauty. "Yes, I am."

He paused to take it all in. "How far along?"

She set aside her glass. He moved his, too. "Three months. The pregnancy calculator says the baby will be here in November."

Happier than he could ever remember being, he pulled her over onto his lap. They shared a tender, celebratory kiss. When it finally ended he held her close, soaking in her warmth, gentleness and strength. The joy between them was as strong as their love.

"In case you haven't noticed, I'm thrilled," he said, finally managing to get the words out.

She returned his smile cheerfully. "I'm over the moon, too. About this. And the fact I finally have a family of my own. And the Welcome Ranch to call home." She hitched in an emotional breath. Tears of bliss suddenly shimmered in her green eyes. "Because it has been that to me, you know."

From the first moment she had set foot on it.

"And it always will be our home," he promised, kissing her again, sweetly and thoroughly this time. "Not just now, but forever."

* * * * *

COMING NEXT MONTH FROM

(H) HARLEQUIN
SPECIAL EDITION

#3031 BIG SKY COWBOY
The Brands of Montana • by Joanna Sims
Charlotte "Charlie" Brand has three months, one Montana summer and Wayne Westbrook's help to turn her struggling homestead into a corporate destination. The handsome horse trainer is the perfect man to make her professional dreams a reality. But what about her romantic ones?

#3032 HER NEW YORK MINUTE
The Friendship Chronicles • by Darby Baham
British investment guru Olivia Robinson is in New York for one reason—to become the youngest head of her global company's portfolio division. But when charming attorney Thomas Wright sweeps her off her feet, she wonders if another relationship will become collateral damage.

#3033 THE RANCHER'S LOVE SONG
The Women of Dalton Ranch • by Makenna Lee
Ranch foreman Travis Taylor is busy caring for an orphaned baby. He doesn't have time for opera singers on vacation. Even bubbly, beautiful ones like Lizzy Dalton. But when Lizzy falls for the baby *and* Travis, he'll have to overcome past trauma in order to build a family.

#3034 A DEAL WITH MR. WRONG
Sisterhood of Chocolate & Wine • by Anna James
Piper Kavanaugh needs a fake boyfriend pronto! Her art gallery is opening soon and her mother's matchmaking schemes are in overdrive. Fortunately, convincing her enemy turned contractor Cooper Turner to play the role is easier than expected. Unfortunately, so is falling for him...

YOU CAN FIND MORE INFORMATION ON UPCOMING HARLEQUIN TITLES, FREE EXCERPTS AND MORE AT HARLEQUIN.COM.

HSECNM1223

Get 3 FREE REWARDS!

We'll send you 2 FREE Books plus a FREE Mystery Gift.

FREE Value Over **$20**

Both the **Harlequin® Special Edition** and **Harlequin® Heartwarming™** series feature compelling novels filled with stories of love and strength where the bonds of friendship, family and community unite.

YES! Please send me 2 FREE novels from the Harlequin Special Edition or Harlequin Heartwarming series and my FREE Gift (gift is worth about $10 retail). After receiving them, if I don't wish to receive any more books, I can return the shipping statement marked "cancel." If I don't cancel, I will receive 6 brand-new Harlequin Special Edition books every month and be billed just $5.49 each in the U.S. or $6.24 each in Canada, a savings of at least 12% off the cover price, or 4 brand-new Harlequin Heartwarming Larger-Print books every month and be billed just $6.24 each in the U.S. or $6.74 each in Canada, a savings of at least 19% off the cover price. It's quite a bargain! Shipping and handling is just 50¢ per book in the U.S. and $1.25 per book in Canada.* I understand that accepting the 2 free books and gift places me under no obligation to buy anything. I can always return a shipment and cancel at any time by calling the number below. The free books and gift are mine to keep no matter what I decide.

Choose one:
☐ **Harlequin Special Edition** (235/335 BPA GRMK)
☐ **Harlequin Heartwarming Larger-Print** (161/361 BPA GRMK)
☐ **Or Try Both!** (235/335 & 161/361 BPA GRPZ)

Name (please print)

Address   Apt. #

City   State/Province   Zip/Postal Code

Email: Please check this box ☐ if you would like to receive newsletters and promotional emails from Harlequin Enterprises ULC and its affiliates. You can unsubscribe anytime.

Mail to the **Harlequin Reader Service:**

IN U.S.A.: P.O. Box 1341, Buffalo, NY 14240-8531
IN CANADA: P.O. Box 603, Fort Erie, Ontario L2A 5X3

Want to try 2 free books from another series? Call 1-800-873-8635 or visit www.ReaderService.com.

*Terms and prices subject to change without notice. Prices do not include sales taxes, which will be charged (if applicable) based on your state or country of residence. Canadian residents will be charged applicable taxes. Offer not valid in Quebec. This offer is limited to one order per household. Books received may not be as shown. Not valid for current subscribers to the Harlequin Special Edition or Harlequin Heartwarming series. All orders subject to approval. Credit or debit balances in a customer's account(s) may be offset by any other outstanding balance owed by or to the customer. Please allow 4 to 6 weeks for delivery. Offer available while quantities last.

Your Privacy—Your information is being collected by Harlequin Enterprises ULC, operating as Harlequin Reader Service. For a complete summary of the information we collect, how we use this information and to whom it is disclosed, please visit our privacy notice located at corporate.harlequin.com/privacy-notice. From time to time we may also exchange your personal information with reputable third parties. If you wish to opt out of this sharing of your personal information, please visit readerservice.com/consumerschoice or call 1-800-873-8635. **Notice to California Residents**—Under California law, you have specific rights to control and access your data. For more information on these rights and how to exercise them, visit corporate.harlequin.com/california-privacy.

HSEHW23